FINDING
LOVE'S FUTURE

FINDING LOVE'S FUTURE

•

Shelley Galloway

AVALON BOOKS
NEW YORK

PRINTED IN THE UNITED STATES OF AMERICA
ON ACID-FREE PAPER
BY HADDON CRAFTSMEN, BLOOMSBURG, PENNSYLVANIA

In loving memory of my father, Barry Galloway.
You would have liked Joanne, Dad.

Special thanks to Kathy Bare, the Loveland Historical Society,
and Dr. Betsy Sabga for their invaluable information.
Any discrepancies are entirely my own.

Chapter One

When Joanne Reece couldn't find a parking place in front of Dr. Whitman's office, she knew that her streak of bad luck wasn't over yet.

"Honestly," she sighed. "You'd think things would get easier one of these days." After finally finding a spot several blocks away, she wearily climbed out of her perky little red Mazda and began the two-block walk to the doctor's office on foot. Well, to say it was walking would be generous. It was more of a hobble, since it was only on one foot. Her left was pretty much out of commission, except for her big toe, which made for a long journey.

The pain made her feel snippy. "Of course there's no parking place near the office," Joanne mumbled to herself. "That would be too simple." She winced as she stepped on the pad of her foot, then continued on, determined. It wasn't easy. A few cracks in the cement made the narrow walkway uneven, and the patches of grass that had found their way through the crevices provided another obstacle. These things turned what had been once just a place to walk into a hazard zone. Joanne found herself gazing at the ground instead of the gorgeous July day.

The aggravation of this little jaunt brought her close to tears. It was her own fault that she was hurting so badly; she should have made time to see Doc two days ago. Honestly, when were things going to start to get better?

Wryly, she imagined that she wasn't the only one to wonder. After all, how much patience could anyone have with her these days . . . especially since she seemed to be in a perpetual blue mood?

Joanne imagined what else could happen to her during this bad luck streak. Break her arm? Cause a minor epidemic? Wreck her car? "My life is a total mess," she mumbled.

Mr. Jensen looked at her strangely from the metal chair on his front porch. "Joanne," he said, nodding.

She blushed; Mr. Jensen must have heard her mumbling. "Hey, Mr. Jensen," she called with a half-hearted wave, then returned her gaze to the sidewalk, aware more than ever that she had probably been the topic of gossip in the town for the last few weeks. Everybody seemed to know that she had lost everything when her antique shop burned down. And, to make matters worse, everybody also seemed to know that she wasn't handling it very well.

Something good had to happen, soon. She needed to cheer up and move on with her life. So what if everything in her life had gone wrong and everyone knew it? It was time for a change.

Joanne winced again as she limped into the doorway of Dr. Whitman's office, and considered the state of her foot once again. At first the wound from the nail hadn't seemed that bad, but now the puncture on the pad of her foot ached like the devil. The skin around the puncture looked angry and swollen. The first thing out of the old doctor's mouth was going to be a reprimand that she should have come in a week ago, when the accident happened.

But there had been so much more than a cut from a rusted nail to worry about. Not only had her wonderful antique shop burned down, but she had lost everything in her apartment above it, too. And then there had been the constant stream of insurance adjusters, police, and fire department officials to deal with. She'd been so overwhelmed. Functioning like a robot, she had gone from one appointment to the next, doing exactly what they told her to do: itemize her losses; put into words what it felt like to lose everything she had; estimate how much money she was entitled to.

And that had been without even putting into account the small fact that she now had no place to live, no job, and no belongings other than those that had been in her overnight bag when the fire broke out. The scrape on her foot had been at the bottom of her priority list.

Joanne signed her name on the paper the receptionist, Mrs. McCluskey, had out for patients.

"Hi, Mrs. Mac," she said pleasantly, determined not to let her blue mood show.

The elderly lady looked up from her latest murder mystery. "Joanne," she said matter-of-factly. "Nice to see you here, *again*."

Greetings done, Joanne limped to the nearest chair. There were two other people in the waiting room, both older gentlemen whom she had known since grade school.

"How's the wait today?" she whispered to the man closer to her.

He shrugged his thin shoulders. "Not too bad. Fair to middlin'."

Mrs. McCluskey harrumphed without looking up from her book.

Joanne shared a smile with the men, but couldn't get her thoughts to turn from the nightmare of the last few days.

While in Columbus at an estate sale, she had received an urgent call from her parents, reporting the news about the fire. The fire investigators said an old electrical circuit had gone bad, sparked, and set the whole building on fire. Because no one had been there, by the time it had been reported to the fire department, Joanne's little building was literally up in flames.

She had immediately driven home and wandered through the rubble as soon as it had been safe to do so—against everyone's better judgment. It was then that she had stepped on an old nail—as well as realized that at twenty-five years old, she was going to be forced to start over.

It had been so hard to swallow. She had put her heart and soul into that store, and experienced a large, gratifying amount of pride from its success. It was a crowning achievement for someone who had always been acknowledged to be book smart, but lacking in common sense. Now what was she going to do? Opening a new shop with no merchandise seemed too dismal a prospect to contemplate.

The nurse appeared then, and Joanne made her way back to the assigned room. After taking off her sock, she relayed her story to Mary, the nurse.

Mary looked carefully at the infected area and grimaced. "That sure looks nasty, Joanne. You should have come in days ago for treatment."

Joanne smiled at her reprimand. "I know, Mary, but with everything going on . . . Besides, I had a tetanus shot a few years ago, remember?"

Mary fingered through Joanne's chart. "How could I forget? You came in for that three years ago, when you got scraped while hiking." The nurse smiled. "You sure were a mess."

Joanne reddened at the memory. She vaguely recalled yelping rather loudly in Dr. Whitman's ear when he bandaged her leg and hands, and then administered the injection. Of course, that hadn't been nearly as bad as when she had fainted on the floor when her blood had been drawn. It was slightly embarrassing to be known through the office as a high-maintenance type of patient. "Doc will know what to do. I bet he won't even be surprised that I've waited this long to come by."

"Ordinarily, I think you would be right about that, but Doc isn't here today." A cautious expression crept onto Mary's face. "I hate to be the one to tell you this, but Doc has a new associate."

"What?" Wariness seeped in. "What happened?"

"Doc's been having some trouble with his asthma. After thirty years he's finally decided to take his own advice and get some help. Dr. Sawyer just joined him last week."

"Dr. Sawyer?" Joanne said, dismayed. "I don't know anything about him. Where did he come from? I'm not going to see *him*, am I?"

Mary looked apologetic. "Now, Joanne, don't get yourself all worked up."

Panic coursed through her. "Mary, you know how anxious I get in here. I can barely come in for a checkup without causing a scene."

"Jo . . ."

"I personally don't think this new guy is ready for me. How old is he? Is he just out of residency?"

Mary was obviously trying to hide a smile. "Around thirty or so."

That didn't sound old enough to her. "Mary, I need someone *competent*. A doctor who can deal with someone like *me*! Please go tell Doc that I'm here. He wouldn't want to subject this new doctor to me. I bet he'll want to come in and see me himself."

"I'm sorry, but we're not taking requests right now," a warm masculine voice said.

Warily Joanne turned her head toward the door. There stood the most beautiful man she had ever seen. Dark hair, blue eyes, strong jaw, broad shoulders. "Oh," she said dumbly.

The doctor, dressed in khakis and a faded blue button-down, strode in, looking relaxed and amused by her tirade. "I'm Stratton Sawyer. I'm sorry I'm not who you want, but I promise I'll do my best, even with someone like *you*."

Joanne felt her cheeks heat as she realized that he had obviously heard quite a bit of her earlier conversation. "You're whom I want," Joanne said automatically, then stopped, appalled by Mary's answering grin. "No, I mean, I'm sorry you overheard my conversation. It's just that I don't do very well at the doctor's office. Dr. Whitman is used to me."

"Used to you?"

Joanne wondered how she could describe herself

without scaring him or becoming completely embarrassed. "I guess you could describe me as a high-
maintenance kind of girl."

Interest flashed in his eyes. "Is that right?"

Dr. Sawyer nodded to Mary, who responded with a
grin and then walked out, leaving the two of them
alone together. He stepped forward and glanced at
Joanne's foot with concern.

She could smell his fresh aftershave. It reminded
her of the woods, and hiking outdoors. She swallowed
hard, and suddenly wished that she had thought ahead
and painted her toenails.

"So, why do you have a fear of doctors?" he asked
as he gently touched the swollen pad of her foot again.

She eyed him cautiously. "It's not a fear of doctors;
it's just of the things that they do to me."

"You've had some bad experiences?" He stepped
away, then opened her chart and began to skim
through her past history.

"Not necessarily. I guess I just get a little too nervous about everything, that's all." Joanne paused,
wondering how she could describe herself without
sounding completely obnoxious. "Um, I've never been
an ideal patient by any stretch of the imagination. I'm
sure if you asked Doc, he'd tell you about the time
when I was twelve and cried because I had to get
another set of shots. Or when I was fifteen and needed
stitches on my arm and cried hysterically the whole
time."

Dr. Sawyer raised his eyebrows. "Oh?"

For some reason, like a reformed Pinocchio, she was compelled to tell the whole truth. "I think the nurse had to hold me down the whole time, too. And, ah, I recall I kicked Dr. Whitman." She glanced at the doctor. Amusement, rather than disdain, crossed his features.

"I'm rambling, I'm sorry." She slung her foot out toward him, barely stopping two inches from his groin. Dr. Sawyer stepped back in alarm. "I'm here about my foot."

"Obviously," he said. "Well, let's take a better look at it then."

He clasped her instep gently and then touched the swollen area in several directions. Joanne bit her lip to keep from crying out. "You've got a pretty good infection here, Joanne."

She nodded. "I've been soaking it in some salt water, but it's only getting worse and worse. When I saw the red lines coming out of it today I figured that I better come in and let you take a look."

His blue eyes twinkled. "Good idea." He touched the rest of her foot, turned it slightly, and examined her ankle and calf. "I don't think it's spread too far yet, but if you hadn't come in, I think it would have been just a matter of time before it would have made you really sick."

"I know I don't need a tetanus shot."

Dr. Sawyer picked up her chart and studied the

notes on the first two pages. "You're right. Your chart says you had one three years ago. We'll just need to put some salve on the cut, bandage it up for a few days, and you'll have to try to stay off of it. Can you do that?"

"Sure," Joanne said, relieved. "I was so afraid you were going to give me a shot."

"Oh, I am. The infection is so far gone that I think you'll need to get an injection right away. We'll also need to clean out the wound. You might have some dirt or something lodged in there."

Joanne felt queasy. "Are you sure?"

"Positive. Why don't you just lie down, and Mary and I will take care of it for you?"

Within minutes, every worry Joanne had ever had about doctor visits materialized. Mary trotted in with a silver tray full of things she couldn't bear to look at, especially after she noticed that a mean-looking syringe was one of the items.

The cleaning of the wound was extremely painful, but it was nothing compared to the apprehension that she felt about the shot. It made her queasy just to think about it coming into contact with her skin.

"Where are you, ah, going to inject that shot, Dr. Sawyer?"

He looked surprised that she had to ask. "In your rear, Joanne," he said matter-of-factly.

The room began to spin. "I don't know . . . how about my arm?"

"It's too big."

Spots of black, then white flashed before her eyes. "My rear's too big?" Then she glanced at the needle and the room began to spin faster.

Stratton looked at her strangely. "We better get this over with." His voice was firm and business-like. "Roll to your side for a moment."

She felt Mary edge down the elastic of her shorts and underwear, felt the cold cotton ball full of alcohol. "Ugh," she groaned.

And that was the last thing she said before she passed out.

Mary and Dr. Sawyer stared at her, surprised.

"At least she's on the table," Mary said matter-of-factly. "You should have seen what a mess she made when she fell down on the stack of charts last time."

Stratton looked at Joanne. "We might as well get this over with before she wakes up. Do you have the penicillin ready?"

"Yes, Doctor."

He took the proffered needle, injected it, and then stood up and set about reviving his patient. "Joanne," he said, waving a small amount of ammonia under her nose.

"Urgg?" She opened one eye.

A grin spread across his face. "I don't believe I've ever heard someone grunt with so much emotion before."

Joanne looked at him quizzically and tried to focus. "I guess I ought to let you know that not only am I high-maintenance, I'm also multi-talented."

He laughed. "Ah. A girl who knows her strengths and weaknesses. I can't wait to get to know you better."

Maybe it was his words, or perhaps it was his kind tone, but no matter what, Joanne felt an attraction toward him like nothing that she had felt before. Suddenly, all of the mess in her life didn't seem quite so bad. Suddenly, she was aware of a little ray of hope creeping into her consciousness. It felt familiar and welcome.

Joanne forced herself to sit up. "Dr. Stratton Sawyer," she said sincerely, "I can't wait, either."

Chapter Two

Stratton figured having the woman of his dreams faint while he was giving her a shot was a sign. Of what, he wasn't sure—but it had to mean something. From the reception area, he watched her leave after speaking briefly with Mrs. Mac, and then stared at the door for a moment. Joanne Reece was just the girl for him. Pretty, redheaded, chatty, cute. He knew without a doubt that he wanted to know her better.

At the moment he didn't care that she was afraid of doctors, and, according to Mary, in the middle of a bad streak of luck. It didn't matter that he couldn't quite understand her train of thought. Also, it was beside the point that he had no business getting romantically involved with someone the first week on the job. Stratton felt it was worth his time to try to figure out the attraction.

As Mary walked over, getting ready to return a few phone calls, he asked, "Do you know Joanne very well?"

She looked up from the chart that she was completing. "Well enough. We were in the same class in high school, and played a few sports together through the years. Like me, Joanne's lived here in Payton all of her life."

"What's she like?"

"Hmm. Well, I'd say people think of her as friendly, kind of dreamy, and a loner."

The odd assortment of adjectives caught him off guard. "Loner? What do you mean?"

She fingered her pencil as she considered. "Well, that probably doesn't describe her well. Let's see. I guess you could call her more of an independent spirit. Never dated anyone real seriously, never tried to fit in with the crowd. She's always just kind of done her own thing."

"Is that a bad thing around here, around Payton?"

Mary smiled at the question. "Oh no, of course not. Everybody loves Jo. Just, that it's such a shame about what happened recently with her house and shop and all."

"She lost everything?"

Mary nodded. "Just about. Luckily, most of her family lives here. She's moved in with her parents, and she has a brother and sister-in-law who don't live more than a mile from this office. I heard she was going to lay low for a little while until she gets her life back together."

"Is she dating anyone?"

Mary gave him a knowing look. "No, not that I know of. I heard she was dating one guy pretty seriously, but I think that ended when her house burned down."

"Why's that?"

"You would have to know this guy to understand. He's a piece of work."

"He sounds like a loser. What's his name?"

"Payton Chase."

Stratton grinned. "Like the town? What's he like?"

"Don't worry, Dr. Sawyer," Mary said cryptically. "Sooner or later, you'll meet Payton. He'll make sure of it. His parents named him after the town because his family was one of the founders."

"What does he do?"

"I guess you could best describe it as dabbling in the family business," she said sarcastically. "He goes to work when he's not playing golf or traveling."

"You don't like him much?"

"I've known him all of my life," she amended. "After all these years, there's really nothing about him to like or dislike." She shrugged. "Payton's just kind of there. As I said, you'll understand when you meet him."

He hoped so. "You said he broke up with her . . ."

Mary placed her group of files on the table. "Payton likes to be seen with people who matter. He's got an inflated sense of self-worth and likes being around the same type of person. Even though Joanne is known as kind of flighty and accident prone, she was also valedictorian of our high school class and homecoming queen. I think Payton thought she was perfect for him. But when Jo's business burned down, she was inconsolable for a few days."

Mary brushed a strand of blond hair back from her eyes. "I mean, she lost just about everything. It would have shaken anybody up. But I think for some reason, it lowered her value in Payton's eyes. She wasn't the girl to be envied anymore, just pitied."

Stratton couldn't fathom Payton's reaction to Joanne's misfortune. Stratton thought again of how she fainted in his office and then tried to pretend that it happened all the time. "I don't think pity would be a word I would ever use to describe her."

"Most people feel the same way. I wouldn't worry about her too much, Dr. Sawyer. Joanne Reece has a way of getting through life just fine."

Stratton thought about their conversation later that afternoon when he was running on the nature path through town. Most people didn't know him yet, so he was allowed to jog in relative silence, only waving to the occasional passerby.

Poor thing, losing everything and then her boyfriend

to boot. What a jerk. He hated the thought of someone being intentionally cruel to another person.

Never in his life could he remember losing everything. Perhaps it was because he started from so little. His parents had both worked in a factory in the small town he grew up in near Cleveland.

His life revolved around their shifts and making do, with his brother and sister. They had learned early in life not to complain too loudly. After all, there was no one around who could have made things better. He had known from a young age that his parents were doing the best they could. If he wanted something different, then it was going to be up to him to make it that way.

So he had tried. He had excelled in track and field, and was able to earn a partial scholarship to a small junior college. Then, he continued to push and push to make things happen. A professor there had seen how driven he was and pulled a couple of strings to get him a full scholarship into Ohio State. From there, he began the agonizing process of trying to get to medical school at the University of Cincinnati.

Somehow, it had all worked out. He had done very well as a resident. He had somehow survived on ramen noodles, cans of vegetables, and little sleep. And six months ago, when Dr. Whitman, one of his mentors, had approached him about a partnership, Stratton had jumped at the chance.

Working in this small practice in Payton was the

realization of his dreams. He wanted to be a family physician. He wanted to be a part of the pulse of a town.

After years of being a latch-key kid, hardly ever seeing both of his parents home on any day except Sunday, he was looking forward to building a relationship with people of all generations. He figured he had been alone too long. He was ready to belong to someone, or something. Payton, Ohio seemed like his best opportunity.

The focus of his thoughts was at the very moment making her way back to her parents' home, all the while wondering how she could have made such a big fool of herself in front of the new doctor.

Had it really been necessary to tell him her whole medical history? Or prepare him to see her at her worst? Or go ahead and faint on him during that nasty shot? Joanne suspected some five-year-olds behaved better on an office visit than she just had.

As she turned into her parents' driveway, her mother stepped out to greet her. "Hi, sweetie. That nice Mary from the doctor's office just called. She said the doctor wanted to remind you to stay off your foot for at least twenty-four hours."

Joanne got out of the car with a grimace. "I seem to remember that. Vaguely."

Daphne Reece walked towards Joanne to lend what

little support her five-foot frame could manage. "She said you had a little incident, Jo."

It was impossible not to see the humor in the phrase. "By incident, you mean she told you I fainted?"

"You should have told me you were going to the doctor. I could have rearranged my plans and gone with you."

"I know you would have, Mom," Joanne said as patiently as she was able. "But I am twenty-five years old. I don't want to take advantage of you . . . I feel like I already am depending on you for so many things. Just because I'm living here doesn't mean I need to revert back to behaving like a child."

"Well . . ." Daphne's voice drifted off meaningfully as she opened the door and guided her daughter to the comfortable family room, decorated in soft shades of lavender. After Joanne was seated, her mother perched on the ottoman next to Joanne's propped foot.

Joanne knew what that drawn out 'well' meant: fainting in the doctor's office from a shot did not signify the behavior of an adult. Her mother had not endured having five children in six years and lived to tell about every gory detail for nothing. Sometimes Joanne wondered how her mother had survived the constant bouts of morning sickness, back pain, and swollen fingers. Not to mention diapers, tantrums, and petty fights. No matter what, Daphne had still managed to make her husband a healthy, home-cooked dinner every night.

Joanne knew other mothers who might have said those things, choosing to exaggerate their symptoms or accomplishments for sympathy. Not her mom. She really had done those things, and still wore a size six, too. In some ways it was tough having a mother so perfect. There were days when she felt that she was never going to measure up.

"What have you been doing today, Mom?" Joanne said in an attempt to change the subject.

"Marianne and I went to have lunch with Mary Beth."

"How's she doing?" Joanne knew that the year before, when Mary Beth was dating her brother, her mother and Mary Beth's had become good friends. Now that Mary Beth was married to Cameron, it seemed as if she had always been part of their family.

"She's enjoying her summer off from teaching kindergarten and has been fixing up their house a little bit."

"Did you have lunch over there?"

"No, we went to the mall. Marianne knew about a special sale that was going on at the Home Store."

"Oh really?" she said in amusement. Everyone knew that when her mother and Marianne went shopping together, trouble was bound to happen.

Daphne continued. "We got the cutest things for their guest bedroom; darling little bear pillows and a matching throw rug. I'm sure Cameron's going to love them."

"Bear pillows? For the guest bedroom?

Daphne shrugged elegantly, her blond hair bouncing slightly from the motion. "Well, it's only a matter of time . . ."

"Mom."

"I know Cameron said they wanted a large family," she continued dreamily.

"Mom, I don't think . . ." Joanne began.

"I just love babies. I thought your dad and I could convert one of the old bedrooms into a nursery. We could paint it blue . . ."

"Mother," Joanne said firmly, "does Cameron know that you're participating in his family planning?"

Daphne pursed her lips. "Now, Jo, don't be such a spoilsport. There's nothing wrong with planning ahead."

"All right. I'm just saying that I never thought of Cameron as the bear pillow type, that's all."

"He will be," Daphne said with a glint in her eye, then crossed her legs and skillfully switched topics. "Now, what did Dr. Whitman say?"

"He wasn't in. I had to see Dr. Sawyer, his new partner."

"And . . ." Daphne's eyes lit up expectantly.

Before she thought the better of it, Joanne began to gush. "He's awfully cute, Mom. Dark hair, steel-blue eyes, the kind you could get lost in. Broad shoulders."

"But . . ." Daphne made a faint gesture towards her daughter's foot.

Joanne waved a hand. "Oh, I know what you're thinking. How could I even be thinking about another guy at a time like this? I shouldn't be thinking about men! I should be thinking about my future. I mean, it's only been a little over a week since Payton dumped me." Joanne rearranged her propped foot more comfortably. "But sometimes you just know, right, Mom?"

Her mother nodded. "Sometimes you do."

Thinking again of Dr. Sawyer's words, Joanne pressed on. "And there's nothing wrong with that, right?"

"Nothing." Daphne coughed delicately. "Dear, I'll be glad to speak about all of this with you . . . but I just wanted to know what the doctor said about taking care of your foot."

"Oh." Joanne felt her cheeks redden. Her runaway mouth had embarrassed her once again. One day she was going to actually think before speaking. "Um, the directions were to stay off my foot, put on the medicated salve he gave me, take the antibiotics, and go see him again in about week."

Daphne stood up. "Well, all right then. We better follow those instructions. Are you hungry?"

"A little."

"I just happened to have made a poppyseed cake this morning. I'll go get you a slice." Daphne's metallic shoes clipped across the tiled floor. "Oh, and I think I'll go make us a nice batch of iced tea. This weather is so oppressive, don't you think?"

"It is hot. Thanks, Mom." Joanne watched her mother walk towards the kitchen and then picked up the day's paper from the coffee table.

Payton's paper was only published twice a week, but that was often enough to keep the residents up to date with the latest news.

Joanne scanned the sports section and smiled as she learned that little league baseball was in full swing and that the high school varsity football team had begun training camp.

After she read that there was going to be a reunion for the Class of '76, a small article at the bottom of the Metro section caught her eye. It seemed the old Jackson house by the train tracks had just been put up for sale. Joanne was glad of that. The house, though once attractive, had been vacant for at least the past five years. She recalled the last owner had moved to a retirement village in Florida. It would be nice to see the Jackson house return to its former glory.

But then her eyes narrowed as she continued to read the short article. Only the land the house was on was being touted as worthy of interest. What if someone just tore it down? That would be a real shame. Hadn't she read somewhere that the Jackson House had historical significance? Joanne seemed to recall rumors that the home had once been a station in the Underground Railroad during the Civil War. *Someone ought to look into that before they just tear the whole thing down,* Joanne thought to herself.

She closed her eyes and remembered walking by the old house when she was a little girl. It had been rundown and in need of a few coats of paint even back then. But, if it had really been an Underground Station . . . wasn't it worth the effort to try to save it?

She looked at her foot. She ought to do some reading about that house since she had some spare time. There had to be something that she could do.

Her mom returned then, bearing two glasses of iced tea and the *TV Guide.* "I've got just the thing to cheer you up, Joanne," Daphne chirped.

"What's that?"

"A Doris Day, Rock Hudson film festival is on cable today."

Joanne bit back a sigh. She had no problem with Doris Day—in fact, she rather liked those old movies—but knowing she had no choice but to watch them left her feeling helpless.

She held up the newspaper. "Mom, did you read this article about the Jackson place? I'm really worried about it."

But Daphne had already turned on *Pillow Talk.* "Oh, look dear, there's Doris in her office. Don't you love her hats?"

Joanne glanced at the screen. Doris did look cute. Really cute, actually. Joanne didn't think she had ever looked that cute in her entire life. "The hats are great.

Doris looks great. As a matter of fact, I don't know why Doris complains about having to share a phone line with Rock Hudson in the first place," she said with more force than she had intended.

Daphne looked as if she was about to explain the plot, then only sighed and patted her daughter on the knee. "Don't worry, dear. Before you know it, you'll be productive again, too."

Joanne flinched at the words. She loved her mother dearly, and knew she hadn't tried to sound judgmental, but Joanne couldn't help but take it that way. It was time to stop feeling sorry for herself and claim her independence back. She knew her mother was trying to help, but she didn't want to go to any more society meetings, or watch old movies in the middle of the day. She wanted a job that she could care about and to be able to go to the doctor without knowing that her mother would hear all about it.

Maybe a start would be to look into the history of the Jackson house, or maybe even get a little part-time job. As Joanne watched Doris fend off Tony Randall, she tore out the article in the paper. As soon as her foot healed, it was time to move on. She needed to reclaim her self-confidence and her sunny disposition. She needed to start looking forward to each new day again.

The resolve made her relax against the cushions and enjoy the movie after all. She smiled as Doris danced with the college boy and then finally made eye contact with Rock. The electricity between them was so fierce that Joanne couldn't help but sigh.

Her mother was obviously thinking the same thing. "Oh, look Jo. Rock's about to pretend he's from Texas! Don't you just love this part?"

Joanne glanced at her mother and grinned. It was impossible to not share her mother's enthusiasm. It was also impossible to forget that she'd had a first meeting of her own that day. Had there been a spark between her and Stratton, too? She liked to think that there had been.

Then, realizing that her mother was waiting for a reply, she spoke. "I love that part, too, Mom," Joanne said finally. "I think it's my favorite."

Chapter Three

"I've got to get out of here, Patty," Joanne stated a week later with a sigh as she leaned back against the serviceable black vinyl chair in her best friend's office. She had decided to spend the afternoon at Temps Are Us after a particularly long morning of meetings with her mother's Symphony Guild.

There were only so many hours in her life that she cared to listen to the merits of table decorations. And she figured that after today, they were all used up. It wasn't that the flowers weren't pretty, or that she faulted the ladies for their interest . . . it just wasn't for her.

So, she had sought refuge in Patty's office, hoping to get inspired into making a decision about her future. Patty was one of the most driven people she had ever known, and therefore perfect for Joanne's interests today.

Joanne waved a hand. "I need more than this."

Patty looked around her spacious office with surprise. "What are you talking about?"

"You know exactly what I meant. I've got to get out of here." She took a minute, realized how she sounded, and then amended her words. "At least out of my parents' house. I need to get back on my feet and move on."

Patty continued the letter she was typing. "How is your foot, by the way?"

Joanne glanced at her foot, now encased in a tennis shoe. "Better, thanks. After sitting around the house for a week, it feels good as new. Um, how's your business doing?"

"Good." Patty slowly looked up from her computer screen as a look of alarm crossed her freckled face. "Why do you ask?"

"Well, I was sort of hoping that I could help you out for a while, until I decide what to do."

Patty's hands stilled on her keyboard. "Gee Joanne, I don't think I need any help right now."

Joanne narrowed her eyes. For some reason, Patty's frown didn't look quite genuine. "I don't mean right here in your office; I mean around town. I could take a couple of temp jobs. It would be fun."

"I don't know . . ."

"Patty!"

Patty's lips pursed. "Um, Joanne, I don't mean to sound rude, but you do have a habit of getting into accidents . . ."

"Oh, come on."

"I just would hate for anything to go wrong, that's all," her friend added weakly.

"I'm good with people," Joanne said quickly. "Everyone knows me. It would be fun."

Patty coughed. "Some of these jobs are anything but fun, Jo. In fact, the openings that I have right now are just plain boring," Patty said matter-of-factly. "You'd be watching the time, hoping for five o'clock every day."

"That wouldn't be a problem. I've been doing that at home for free. I could definitely handle getting paid to watch the clock."

"I suppose."

"What do you have now?"

"Not much," Patty hedged as she turned from her computer to look down at the list of openings on the corner of her desk.

"There's got to be something . . ."

"Well, actually, there is one job I think you might like. It involves working down at the Envirovision building. They need someone to help copy documents, compile packets, and send out mailers. Pretty boring stuff, but then again, it's only for a week."

"That's okay. I'll take boring any day. I need to get back on my feet, literally."

Patty looked unsure. "Um, the owner is pretty particular about how she wants things done."

Joanne knew that she would need to do everything and anything to get her life back in order. "Pat, I'll do my best. That's all anyone can ask for, right?"

"That's true," Patty said thoughtfully as she stared at the form. "Actually, I don't think there's any way that you could get into trouble there."

Joanne wasn't impressed with Patty's lack of enthusiasm. "Honestly, Patty, you'd think I was some kind of criminal."

Her friend turned to look at Joanne directly, her blue eyes sharp and aware. "Temps Are Us needs all the business it can get. I have to be careful."

Joanne knew exactly what Patty was not saying. Still, it didn't make it any easier. It was hard to realize that even her best friend had doubts about her capabilities. She retorted by making light of her feelings. "Why are you being like this? Are you still obsessing about our prom night?"

"That was years ago."

"I know you though. You've got a mind like an elephant."

Patty reddened. "Now Jo, I had forgotten all about how you ruined my dress the moment we walked into the restaurant, two hours before the dance."

"It wasn't my fault that the waiter ran into me." Joanne scanned her friend's face, looking for answers. "Is it the Christmas tree?"

"I would never hold that over you for ten years,"

Patty said. "But, you *were* the one that knocked it over and broke my mother's antique ornament."

"I thought everyone agreed that *anybody* could have run into that tree. It was in the middle of your entryway."

"But no one ever had, until you did on Christmas Eve." Patty coughed slightly. "All I'm saying is that wherever you go, accidents are sure to follow."

"Nothing's happened lately, Patty."

"Well, I seem to recall that your shop just burned down," her friend deadpanned.

Patty did have her there. "Excuse me, but that was three weeks ago."

Patty flashed a smile. "My point exactly."

"Patricia Anne, I don't see how a string of bad luck should interfere with my ability to be a good temp."

Patty grinned and held her hands up in mock horror. "I hate it when you use my full name. It's like I'm back in first grade. I can't take it any more!" She took a deep breath. "All right. Fine. You win. Give this job a try, but don't say I didn't warn you when you realize just how tedious it is."

Joanne let out a deep breath that she hadn't realized she had been holding. "Great. I'll be glad to help you out. When do I start?"

"Tomorrow, if you could. I'll call them later and tell them to expect you, and then give you the paperwork to fill out."

*   *   *

Thirty minutes later, Joanne walked out, pleased with the beginning of her new vocation: temporary worker. Sure, it wasn't much, if you compared it to the satisfaction of owning her own business . . . but it suited her purposes for the time being. She could get out of the house, make a little bit of money, and use the time to plan for her future. Maybe she could even do some research about the Jackson house. Someone needed to do some investigating about its history.

As she made her way out of Temps Are Us and meandered toward her favorite coffee shop, she spied Dr. Sawyer. He was dressed casually again—old khakis, white button-down, and scuffed loafers. His black hair glinted in the sun. He looked terrific. It also looked as though he favored cappuccinos in the afternoon too. "Hi there, Dr. Sawyer. Remember me?" she asked cheerily.

"How could I forget the first patient to faint on me in Payton?" he replied with a grin.

She felt a blush climb her neck. "I did warn you that I was a little queasy around doctor's offices."

"I only remember that you said you were high-maintenance and multi-talented. Tell me, are you always queasy around doctors, or just in the actual offices?"

"I don't think I'm queasy around doctors all of the time," she said, flustered. "Actually, I'm pretty certain that doctors don't bother me a bit when they're off duty."

His blue eyes met hers. "Would you be willing to have a cup of coffee with me, then?"

As if he had to ask. "Thanks, Dr. Sawyer. I'd love to." She would have had a glass of prune juice, just to be in Stratton Sawyer's company.

He held open the door for her as she passed through. "Please call me Stratton."

"All right, Stratton." Just the sound of his name on her lips made her smile.

After a few minutes of waiting in line, they sat down across from each other at a small table near the window. Joanne motioned towards the glass. The sidewalks were fairly crowded. Women with strollers, kids with ice cream cones, professionals dodging everyone while talking on their cellphones . . . all against a perfect background of blue sky and green trees. It was a perfect spot to people watch. "How do you like our little town?"

"Very much. I've enjoyed the people I've met so far, even though many of them have been disappointed that Dr. Whitman wasn't available. Now, I just need to begin to find my way around the outskirts of Payton and into Cincinnati. It's getting a little old just going to the diner to eat."

"I'll be happy to tell you about some other places to eat, or even take you to a few, if you'd like." She stilled as she heard her words. Did it sound like she was propositioning him? Did it? She swallowed hard.

Blue eyes met hers. Her breath caught in her throat. "Thanks," he said. "I'd like that, Joanne."

A feeling of warmth rushed through her. Flustered, she said, "It's no trouble. Mary has probably told you that I've lived here all of my life."

"I did hear that. I also heard that you're one of five kids and have a lawyer for a father."

Taken aback, she eyed him cautiously. "Gee. Did you learn anything else?"

He leaned back against his chair and brought a foot to rest across his other knee. "I learned that there are a whole lot of people who think highly of you."

She laughed. "Well, I hope that's all they think of me! I'm known as pretty flighty, I think. But it was fun growing up in a house full of kids. What about you? Do you come from a large family, too?"

He shook his head. "I have a brother and a sister. It was just us and my parents."

"There were days in middle school when that sounded pretty good to me," Joanne laughed. "Some days I longed for time to myself."

"I had plenty of that," Stratton replied, a distant look appearing in his expression.

Joanne gazed at him in concern, then resolutely lightened their conversation. "Well, next time we have a family get-together, I'll bring you along. After one long dinner, you'll be longing for some peace and quiet!"

Stratton laughed. "Your family's a little gregarious?"

"You could say that. 'Loud' might be a better description. For the most part we all like to talk a lot. And my parents are fun. My mom is outgoing and my dad is anything but stuffy."

"I'll look forward to meeting them."

His words and proximity caused her pulse to quicken. She could feel the electricity between them, though Stratton didn't seem to feel the need to acknowledge it verbally, either. At a loss for words, Joanne chewed her bottom lip, sipped her cup of coffee, and then finally turned her head to watch the people walk on the sidewalk in front of them.

Several stopped and waved to her. She lifted a hand in response.

Joanne motioned to the two women who were currently passing in front of them. "Have you had a chance to meet Mrs. Frazer or Mrs. Bingham yet?"

Stratton looked uncomfortable. "Well, Mrs. Bingham came in, but once she heard that Dr. Whitman was out, she turned back around and went to the doctor over in Kimberly."

"Didn't Mrs. McCluskey step in and vouch for you?"

He chuckled. "I think Mrs. McCluskey takes her job description very seriously. And unfortunately for me, nowhere on it does it say 'introduce new doctor to suspicious patients'. I'm out of luck."

"What you need is for someone to take you around to the town functions, introduce you to everyone, get you acclimated. Then people will begin to warm up. It just takes time."

"Are you volunteering for that job?"

Taken off guard, Joanne stared at him blankly for a moment, then kicked into action. After all, what did she have to lose? She knew that she wanted to be with him some more. A lot more. "As a matter of fact, I am," she said bravely.

His hand reached out to hers. She shook it, marveling at the gentleness of his clasp, despite the calluses on his palm. Warily she met his expression, afraid he would see how much such a simple gesture affected her. "I think it would be a lot of fun," she said breathlessly.

"Great. What do you have in mind to do first?"

Many activities crossed her mind, none of which had anything to do with other people. She glanced at Stratton; he stared at her intently, waiting for an answer. "Ah, how about dinner with me and my parents tonight?"

"Tonight? Won't they need more warning than a few hours?"

"Actually, no," Joanne replied with a smile. "My mother verges on being perfect. Nothing as inconsequential as an extra person for dinner would throw her off. Besides, we're going to the country club tonight, so she won't mind a bit."

"Country club?"

"Oh, it's not the type of place that you might think. It's pretty casual, and there will be lots of potential patients for you to meet, too. It's, ah, bridge night."

He looked amused. "Will we be playing bridge?"

"Gosh, I hope not. We can skip out of there by the time the tables begin to get set up." She paused for a moment, well aware that she was in danger of rambling again. "How does that sound?" she asked.

Joanne felt vulnerable as she waited for his response. What did he think of her offer? Of her? Every word her mother ever told her about posture came roaring into her brain. Perhaps that would give her some backbone. Joanne willed herself to sit straighter on the barstool. She pulled her shoulders back, then met Stratton's eyes.

He seemed to watch her transformation with interest. A smile played on the edge of his lips. "It sounds perfect, Joanne. I'm looking forward to it."

She exhaled and felt her body relax again. "Oh, me too."

Three hours later, Stratton pulled up to the Reece residence. The house was an old fifties-style ranch, painted a light lemon color, with a cheery red door. It looked like Joanne, although he would be hard-pressed to explain why he felt that way.

He shook his head slightly as he got out of his old BMW and made his way up the sidewalk to the front door. Never in a million years would he have thought he would be getting ready to take the classiest girl he had ever met out to the country club for dinner. The guys back home would get a good laugh out of that. It was a far cry from the way his life had been when he was growing up.

He knocked on the door, and was taken aback when it was instantly opened by a petite blond woman with lovely gray eyes.

"Hello, Stratton?" she asked, one manicured hand extended.

"Yes. Mrs. Reece?"

She nodded. "We're so glad you could join us this evening."

"I'm sorry for the short notice—"

She held up a hand. "Don't think a thing of it. We don't stand on formalities around here."

"Well, then, thank you for having me."

"Any friend of Joanne's is welcome here, any time. Come on in. Jim was just attempting to get the stereo to work."

"Excuse me?"

She stopped and raised her head to meet his six-foot, three-inch gaze. "Are you mechanically inclined, by any chance?"

"Well . . ."

"We had a little accident with this confusing system," she began before he could reply, her heels clicking on the tile as she led the way toward the living room. "A button needs to be pushed so we can hear the speakers, but there's about a dozen to choose from. I think we've completely messed it up," she whispered as they reached the entryway. Obviously it was a sore subject.

Stratton listened to Daphne's speech in wonder. For some reason, he had supposed she would have been grilling him about his background, or praising his occupation—not discussing her stereo as if they were old friends. "I'll see what I can do to help."

As they entered the room, he saw Joanne and her father in the midst of the most elaborate stereo system he had ever seen. At least five components were stacked on top of each other. Several wires snaked out of each. CD's, brochures, and gold, blue, and red wires littered the shelves. And Mr. Reece was pushing each of the twenty buttons systematically.

Jim Reece looked up. "Hey there, Stratton Sawyer. Come over here and give me a hand."

Instantly Stratton was handed a manual. "Read this and tell me what you think," Jim barked good-naturedly.

Stratton scanned the manual but couldn't help himself from focusing on Joanne. She wore a pretty sundress and her beautiful hair was pulled back. She seemed to notice his attention and gave a small wave from her position next to the various controls. "Hi, Stratton," she called out before concentrating once again on her father's directions.

"Press the left button, Jo," Jim called out.

"This one?"

"No, the other one on your left."

"Dad, there's three buttons on the left."

Finally Jim met Stratton's gaze. The older man's eyes were piercing, stern. Stratton imagined they had intimidated quite a few people in the courtroom. "What do you think we should do?" he snapped. "We've been trying to play one song for the last forty-five minutes."

Before he could help himself, Stratton blurted verbatim what was going through his mind. "I think you should go get yourself an easier stereo."

Daphne chuckled; Joanne groaned.

For a moment, Jim just stared at him, then his expression broke into a grin. "I knew I was going to like you, Stratton Sawyer. Come on, let's leave this mess and go get you a beer."

Stratton felt his whole body relax, although he didn't realize it had been tense. He glanced at Joanne. She only gave him a Mona Lisa smile. Finally, he replied to the man who was so different from his father, "That sounds great, Mr. Reece. Thanks. Thanks a lot."

Chapter Four

Payton Country Club had been around for a long time. Built in 1940, it had begun as a social club for ladies who enjoyed tennis and bridge. Several years later a pool was added; then a nine-hole golf course was built. Then another nine holes. Eventually a restaurant and pro shop were added, too.

The country club had a large following in the sixties and a decrease in membership in the seventies. The eighties and nineties brought a resurgence of interest, as well as a children's area and baby pool. The latter was supposedly built for the convenience of young mothers, but everyone knew it was so the old-timers could sit by the pool and not get splashed by the rowdy four-year-olds.

To a first-time visitor, Payton Country Club might

have seemed a little run-down and worn out. Nothing about it looked prestigious, though guidebooks to various clubs said it was. The lawns were manicured, but not excessively, and the clubhouse was in need of remodeling. Of course, it had been in need for years. The furniture had the look of the seventies, and the dark woodwork was outdated. But everyone liked it. A lot.

The membership was eclectic and diverse. The club had never been called exclusive by anyone's estimations, which was exactly how they wanted it. As Stratton looked around the facility for the first time, he knew he liked it the minute he stepped into the entryway with Joanne and her parents.

After giving Stratton a quick tour, Mr. and Mrs. Reece commandeered him as their own. Within minutes he had a beer in one hand and was using his right to shake many others that were proffered. People were friendly and greeted him with an odd mix of warmth and anxiety. He was either listening to advice about living in the town or answering questions about a variety of ailments. But no matter what, he had to admit that he did feel included for the first time since moving to Payton.

"Pleased to meet you, young man," an eighty-year-old gentleman said as Mr. Reece stopped by the bar. "Has anyone told you about my heart problems?"

"No, sir."

Just as the man was about to begin to describe his heart medication, Jim Reece cut him off.

"He's off duty, Art," Jim said gruffly. "That's what office hours are for. Go make an appointment."

Within minutes, the man said he'd do just that, and then walked away. Stratton turned to his liberator. "Thanks, Mr. Reece."

"It's Jim to you. And no problem. Got to watch out, Stratton, or everyone will hit you up for free advice," Jim said seriously. "Take it from a lawyer. That won't do. Need to get paid for your time."

"Yes sir, I'll remember that." As Jim expounded on his theories, Stratton's attention wandered. Joanne was near, in that vivid pink sundress that did amazing things to her coloring. It should have clashed with her auburn tresses, but instead it accentuated her lovely skin. It was difficult not to just stare at her.

As soon as her father became involved in a lengthy discussion with one of the insurance salesmen in town, Joanne took over the tour-guide duties.

"Come on, quick, before my dad drags you over to meet more of his cronies," she teased.

"Whatever you say."

"I'll show you around, but I've got a few people in mind that you might enjoy getting to know."

Stratton's blue eyes met hers. "Like I told you earlier, I'm all yours."

Joanne's pulse quickened, and she stared at him dumbly, the words echoing in her mind. Had he really said that? Suddenly she couldn't remember. What did it mean, that he was all hers?

"Joanne?"

"Oh, I'm sorry, I guess my mind just drifted off for a second. Let's go say hi to Julie and Matt."

Within a few minutes, Joanne led Stratton over to a couple that she had gone to high school with, an older lady named Millicent Peters, a pair of young parents who spoke only of their baby's bout with colic, and finally to the McKinleys, her semi-in-laws. Mr. McKinley looked pleased to meet someone new.

"So you're the new doctor everybody's been talking about," Baron McKinley said as he clasped Stratton's hand in a death grip.

"Yes, sir. I hear you're related to Joanne."

"That's a fact. Her brother married my daughter Mary Beth. No children yet, though."

"Mr. McKinley, it's only been a year," Joanne interjected.

Joanne thought the look the older man leveled her way was priceless. "Long enough," he groused.

Then Baron changed the subject. "Where are you from, Stratton?"

"Prescott, near Cleveland."

"I spent some time up there briefly," Baron said with a speculative gleam in his eye. "And of course, there's lots of Sawyers in this world . . . would I know your parents? Either of them in sales?"

"No, I'm afraid not," Stratton said in an understatement. "They've both passed away, but they were factory workers, not in sales, in the mills near Prescott."

Baron nodded. "Hard work. My father worked in a steel mill for a time."

"Yes, sir."

"It's a shame that you've already lost them." A hint of compassion entered Baron's features. "I'm sure you were proud of them, son, just like they would be proud of you now."

Stratton's ruddy complexion paled. "Thank you, sir."

Just then, Mr. and Mrs. Reece, as well as Baron's wife, Marianne, approached. "Y'all ready for dinner? The buffet line is forming," Jim Reece said with a meaningful nod.

"Ready," Baron said without hesitation.

At Stratton's confused look, Joanne interpreted. "There's never enough roast beef," she said with a smile. "Stragglers get ham."

"Ham," Baron repeated with disdain.

"Well, we better get in line, then."

Joanne clasped his arm as they joined the queue of people. "You hanging in there?"

"Sure. This is fun, Joanne."

"I'm glad you think so. Everyone here can be overwhelming, even for me sometimes."

"I would have never have noticed. You seem to get along with everyone here just fine."

"I do get along well with everyone," she said, then

pursed her lips as her former boyfriend came into view. "Well, I do with *almost* everyone."

Stratton's gaze followed hers.

Joanne knew that she should turn away, but she couldn't seem to stop staring. Payton was wearing his blond hair a little longer than the way she had remembered it. And he was wearing his favorite navy jacket with his made-up family crest on the breast pocket. He also was sporting his usual smug expression. He seemed oblivious to her presence.

"Who's that?" Stratton asked curiously. "That guy in the blue blazer?"

Joanne tried her best to sound nonchalant. "That's um, Payton Chase. I'm sure you'll be hearing about him sooner or later. He's pretty well known in our little town." She finally turned away from Payton and tried to concentrate on the cheesy oil painting that had adorned the wall ahead of them for years, or anything else that would divert Stratton's interest. "Um, would you like me to tell you about the time my parents took us here for dinner when all five kids were under eight?"

Stratton didn't seem to take her hint, only continued to stare at Payton. "I happened to have already heard that you used to know that Payton guy pretty well."

"That's old news," Joanne answered with a strained smile. "We broke up when my place burned down."

"He sounds like a jerk."

"I guess he is." She glanced at Payton again, then turned quickly away when she saw his arm slide possessively around a willowy blond, and then raise his eyes to hers. She swallowed hard. So, Payton *had* known she was there.

Stratton continued the questions. "You guess he is a jerk?" he blurted. "This guy left you just when you needed him most. How can you even doubt that he's an idiot?"

Oh, why did they have to be talking about Payton at all? "Stratton, look at me," she said, deliberately adopting a light tone. "I've got no job, no place to live, and half the time I'm the joke of the town." She gestured with her hands. "I'm always getting into mishaps. The only thing I've ever been really good at is studying the past. Why wouldn't Payton want to look for someone else?"

He didn't seem fooled by her self-deprecating words. Instead, he stepped closer and clasped her arm. "I see a lovely woman standing front of me, Joanne. I see someone who likes to laugh and is well liked by most of the people in this room," he murmured, his voice low and soothing. "You need to give yourself more credit."

"But . . ."

He raised a hand to her lips to stop the rush of words. "All I know is that I'm glad I met you, Joanne, that's all," he said simply. Then, as if realizing that they were just about to the head of the buffet line, he said, "Hey, we're in luck! There's still roast beef."

Joanne smiled at his words. "Dad will be pleased."

The evening flew by. People were seated in groups of four or six, but that didn't seem to matter. Men and women constantly stood up, switched chairs, and joined other tables. Joanne and Stratton took part in several of the exchanges.

Sprinkled in the conversations was talk of the Jackson home. A few people had thought it was a good idea to have the building zone changed, from residential to commercial, so when the Jackson house was torn down, a mini-mart could be built in its place.

Joanne couldn't help but feel alarmed by the talk. She filled Stratton in on what she knew of the Jackson house and its history.

He seemed to understand her dismay. "You ought to do something about that, Joanne," he murmured. "You ought to do a report to the town council about the history of the house before someone tries to change the zone and buy it."

"I agree. *Someone* does, but certainly not me! That project would need someone qualified, with experience in these matters."

Stratton glanced around the crowded room. "Do you see anyone who is volunteering?"

She was saved from replying by the appearance of Dr. Whitman. "How're you doing, Stratton?" he asked, looking smart in a seersucker suit. "It's good to see you here."

Stratton looked pleased to see him. "I'm fine, thanks. Would you like to join us?"

"I would," the elder doctor said, then after exchanging pleasantries with Joanne, seated himself in the empty chair next to Stratton. Within moments, the two men began to discuss the practice.

Relieved at the respite that Dr. Whitman had given her, Joanne was pleased to merely listen to their exchange. Yes, she was interested in the fate of the Jackson House, but it wasn't up to her to actually do something about it, was it? She shook her head slightly and then removed all thought of the house from her mind. There were plenty of other things to occupy her thoughts at the moment, the least of which being the man who was seated to her left.

The evening continued in a blur for Stratton. After he finished conversing with Dr. Whitman, he was content to merely observe the people in the room. It looked as if the couples were performing some care fully orchestrated dance and he enjoyed watching the interplay of a group of people who had known each other for decades. Slights and triumphs were recalled with enough precision to make a casual listener believe they had only happened yesterday.

Besides medical school, he had never been part of a group that had such a common bond with each other, perhaps because where he grew up, no one could afford that luxury. Most were merely just trying to scrape out a living. There had been no time to dwell on the Petersons' new car, or the Fouzers' marriage, or the interest of the new doctor in the town.

Once they warmed up to him, Stratton was amazed that these people genuinely seemed to care about his happiness, and didn't just look at him with distrust. Of course, a lot of the credit was due to his escort. Joanne knew everyone and seemed to be a favorite.

Through it all, she stayed by Stratton's side. He enjoyed how everybody seemed to know her, was drawn to her bubbly personality. Most seemed concerned about her welfare, and offered her free advice.

There was a thoughtful silence when many heard about her new job at Temps Are Us, followed by a few sighs of relief when they learned at what office she was due to begin work.

"When do you start?" Stratton asked, as they were getting ready to leave. The bridge competition was forming, and neither of them was eager to give it a try.

"Tomorrow morning." Joanne led the way out the door and thought about what he, a doctor, must think of her new occupation.

"Stratton, if you could have seen my old shop, you would have been impressed. I really put my heart and soul into it. This little job isn't much, but it will help me gain a little time and respect, until I decide what to do next."

"Why don't you just rebuild? I'm sure the insurance would help with the costs."

"It wouldn't be the same. The building was built in 1870. It had thick walls, plastered ceilings, leaky pipes, sloping floors, and history. I can't bear the thought of having an antique shop in a new building. Something about it would seem cheap to me. Like one of those craft places in a strip mall."

"You could—"

"No." She stopped him by placing her forefinger to his lips. "I'm not ready to begin again, Stratton. That's what it really comes down to. I'm not ready to give that much of myself to something inanimate again."

He was stilled by her touch. "I understand."

They began walking again, and as they did so, she gave him a sideways look. "If you do, I'd say you were the first person. So many people have just wanted me to pick myself up and start again—as if I hadn't really lost my whole life's work in one moment. It's been hard to make people understand that I can't just go on, pretend that I don't miss my things, my stuff. I don't know why."

"What about your parents? How do they feel about all of this?"

She laughed. "I think they understand, to some degree. But I also think that there's a part of them that just wants me to move on, out of their house, as quickly as possible. Mom's ready for grandchildren, not prodigal daughters."

He met her gaze. "When I wanted to become a doctor, a lot of people didn't understand it, either. So many thought I was thumbing my nose or something at my parents' and neighbors' way of life." He lowered his voice as he imitated the words he had heard for years. " 'Why isn't the factory good enough for you, boy? Your father works there. It's paying for your food right now.' "

Joanne's eyes softened with compassion. "I bet that was tough."

He ran a hand through his hair. "I don't want your sympathy; I'm just trying to tell you that I know what you're going through, to some extent. I couldn't explain why I wanted to be a doctor so badly. I just knew, in my heart, that it was the right thing for *me* to do."

The couple stepped onto the parking lot, and then Stratton opened the car door for her and held her elbow gently as she stepped inside.

"Where would you like to go now?" he asked.

She had many ideas; none of them appropriate for a tour guide. "I'm happy with anything."

"But you're forgetting that you promised to show me around."

Joanne's mind began to spin. There had to be somewhere interesting to take him at nine at night. Then, after a moment's pause, she knew of the perfect spot. "I have just the place for you."

She took him to a large park next to the Little Miami River. Old-fashioned lights cast a warm glow over the walking paths and fragrant flowerbeds. An open-air amphitheater with stone steps cut into a hill perched in the distance. On Sunday afternoons, the place was crowded. But at this time of night, it was practically vacant.

They stepped out of the car, and Joanne gratefully took his suit jacket that he had laid in the back of the car. Even though the July days were stifling hot, the night brought a chill to the air. As she enfolded herself in the fabric, the scent of his cologne made her shiver. It felt so good to be with him—right, somehow.

They walked along one of the paths, the one that passed the vacant playground and then meandered closer to the banks of the river. They stopped along the edge. The water level was low. The current slapped against the rocks that jutted out from the bottom.

Joanne stepped carefully as they left the path and walked closer to the edge. Stratton held out a steadying hand; she took it gratefully. "This is one of my favorite places."

"Why's that?"

"I guess because it brings back so many memories. I remember picnicking here in grade school and walking along the banks with one or another of my brothers. Sometimes, my dad took us down here when we wanted to fish."

They hiked along the edge, listening to the crickets and pointing out the glow of an occasional firefly. Stratton's thumb rubbed the smooth skin on the back of her hand. "Did you ever catch anything?"

She laughed. "Once I caught a Walkman."

Stratton grinned. "Now, *that's* a fish story."

They walked some more, Joanne pointing out trees, pretty flowers in the dim light, the outline of an owl in the sky. And then they said nothing. It felt as if they were the only ones for miles around. The water rippled next to them, and the frogs seemed to shout in the background. When Joanne stumbled, Stratton slid an arm around her waist to hold her steady. She felt the warmth of his body against her hip. The contact made her breath catch. More than ever she was aware of his presence, his scent, the steady feel of him next to her. She darted a look at his profile. It looked strong and chiseled, so handsome. Had Payton ever made her feel this way? She couldn't remember.

Eventually, they turned and retraced their steps. "This has been nice, Stratton," she said, leaning into his body. "It's been so long since I just relaxed. I love this place."

"When was the last time you were here?"

"Gosh, I don't know. Payton hated coming here. He said it just reminded him of being in high school, and that there were too many bugs and too much mud for his Polo loafers." Joanne tilted her face up to the moonlight, remembering. "Boy, I guess the last time I was here with a guy was my senior year in high school. It was a big place for dates."

A knowing grin crossed Stratton's face. "Good place for parking, hmm?"

She answered with a smile. "Yep. Of course, that was a long time ago."

Stratton's hand brushed back her hair; the weight of it was causing her ponytail to slip. "So, is it too late?"

Her pulse quickened. "Too late? For what?"

"For you to want to kiss someone here."

Her eyes met his as she shook her head slightly. "It's not too late." Then she realized how she must have sounded, so gauche, so . . .

His lips lowered and touched hers tentatively, then again, more demanding. She eagerly responded and raised her hands to his chest, as his own encircled her slim figure.

Then Stratton raised his head. "I think I'm going to like living here, Joanne."

"Me too," she breathed.

He grinned at her words. "I also think I better take you home. You've got a big day tomorrow."

Joanne said nothing as he took her hand and walked back towards his car. There were too many thoughts running through her head to voice any one of them.

And she wasn't sure if she was ready for Stratton to hear any of those thoughts. Suddenly, everything seemed awfully confusing. Too confusing to share, anyway.

Chapter Five

The next morning, Joanne was in the Envirovision office and things were not looking good.

"Joanne, let me be as specific as I can," Deb Afton, the office manager said. "I have a whole pile of documents that need to be copied, collated, made into booklets, and then delivered. In addition, I need another copy to be made for each first page, and then filed, according to the account number on the corresponding form."

Deb eyed Joanne through her wire-rimmed glasses, paused for breath, and then continued. "Now, if there is no account number, you will need to go look it up on the computer. Come see the disks. Do you see how each one is labeled, and how they are stored alphabetically . . . ?"

"Yes," Joanne answered weakly. The instructions continued, but Joanne only grasped every third word. Who knew organizing and sorting papers could be so complicated?

With her eyebrows raised and head tilted, Deb scrutinized her new employee. "Do you understand, Joanne?" she asked in a clipped tone. "If you don't, I'll be glad to go over the instructions again, even help you design note cards to follow."

"No, I'll be just fine. No problem," Joanne responded with more confidence than she felt. She had actually gotten confused an hour ago. That was around the time that Deb had been explaining the phone system. The twenty buttons, complete with voice mail codes, seemed like a lot of trouble when just answering the phone and writing down a message was so easy.

For a moment, Joanne felt a strong longing for her little shop again, where deciding what kind of coffee to brew was always the most important thing on her morning agenda. But how could she verbalize that? How could she tell everyone that what she wanted was her freedom back? That she wanted to feel confident and sure of herself again? There was no good way. And she certainly knew better than to let Deb know her thoughts. Deb would take it as a sign that Jo was incompetent and get worried. There was no way she wanted Deb to feel obligated to explain the directions again. She wasn't ready to be subjected to the alphabetical labeling system again. "I'm ready for any-thing," she added for good measure.

Deb smiled with obvious relief, stood up, and then straightened the skirt of her suit. "Well, that's great, then. I've got to go make a dozen deliveries now, so I'll see you later. Don't forget about the contact num-bers I gave you in case anything goes wrong."

"I gotcha," Joanne said with a mini-salute. "Don't worry about anything. Nothing will go wrong. I'll get busy copying these papers in just a minute."

"Thanks." Deb turned to walk away, but after a mo-ment faced Joanne again. "I just wanted to say, ah, I sure am sorry about your shop. I really enjoyed Sunken Treasures."

"Thank you. I am, too. But life goes on, doesn't it?" Joanne turned away, not ready for Deb to see just how much the loss of her store affected her. "I'm just glad I'll be doing this for a few days. It will be good to get my mind off of things." Like a home, a decent job, and a certain cute doctor who really knew how to kiss.

After a few more minutes of conversation, Deb left, and Joanne was left to stare at least eight piles of pa-per, two pages of addresses, and a very big copy ma-chine. "Hmm," she said, thinking that maybe she should have listened a little more carefully.

But after rereading the neatly typed directions, and spending a few minutes getting organized, Joanne was as ready as ever. Resolutely she began to feed the paper through the machine. As it spit out copies at the bottom, she was reassured, and began her temporary job in earnest.

After two hours, she had one set of packets done and was busily filing when the phone rang. "Hello, this is Envirovision," she said, according to her notes.

"Hi Joanne," Patty said. "How's it going?"

"Great. Piece of cake," Joanne replied as she thumbed through another drawer of file folders. "But between you and me, I think Deb might have a hard time filling this position later on. She's a little neurotic."

"Neurotic? You and I have known her for years, Jo. Why do you say that?"

"Well, she has a space for everything. And it has to be exactly just so," Joanne explained, the hour of instruction still ringing in her ears. "For Deb, there's no margin for error. Actually, in my opinion, her perfectionism is bordering on unhealthy."

"Joanne?" Anxiety filled Patty's voice. "Will you be able to do this, just like she wanted?"

"Of course. I'm just stating my opinion, that's all."

When she hung up, Joanne went back to the grind. Patty had been right; this was not the job for her. She felt like an idiot, trying to do things right but only making them worse. There were too many papers, too many rules, and no one to talk to. She was lonely and tired of alphabetizing. After another few minutes, she knew it was time to get a soda.

She had just poured the Sprite when the phone rang, the copier buzzed, and a stack of papers that had just been neatly stacked slid onto the ground. "Hello," she gasped as she reached for the clear button on the machine. "Oh, Envirovision."

Deb was on the line. "Joanne? Is everything all right?"

"Sure." Joanne pushed the clear button again. A high-pitched squeak began to sound.

"What's that noise?"

"Oh, the copier has just started alarming." Joanne tried to sound calm. "Any idea about what could be the problem?"

"Sounds like a paper jam. Do you see the top, the control panel? What's blinking?"

"Oh, yeah, I see it. It's the paper sign. Don't worry, I'll fix it. Do you need anything?"

"No, I just wanted to make sure you were all right. We're running late. Do you need me to come back?" Deb asked, her voice etched with concern. "Do you need anything?"

Another job, Joanne thought, but only said, "No, everything's under control, but I do need to go and fix this up."

"All right then."

Joanne hung up, reached for the clear button on the copier, and knocked over the can of Sprite. Liquid ran out of the can, and over the pile of completed papers. "Rats!" she muttered.

Such an accident called for immediate action. Papers needed to be picked up, soda needed to be blotted, and the buzzer stopped. Too bad that she couldn't manage any of those at the same time.

It was also too bad that the papers that had just gotten soaked were the ones that needed to be copied. Hurriedly, she found a roll of paper towels, tore a few off, blotted the desk, floor, and papers, and then concentrated on the copier.

The tiny glowing directions on the top made little sense, but somehow she figured out that there was a jam in sections 3, 4, and 5. Great. She pushed clear, and then opened up the various doors of the too-smart machine. Suddenly the alarm quieted. Jo breathed a sigh of relief.

She glanced at the stack of papers and the time on the clock. So much to do, so little time to do it.

Without thinking about what she was doing, Joanne went ahead and laid a Sprite-soaked paper on the glass top to get copied. But then, as if in slow motion, she watched the soggy paper go into the machine sluggishly and then get stuck. This time the alarm sounded louder. Joanne frantically pressed buttons. Lights began to flash. "Oh come on," she snapped to the machine as she pulled open one of the doors. "Enough's enough."

Making an executive decision, Joanne grabbed the first lever in front of her and pulled it down. It clicked into place. The machine groaned loudly, and then finally stilled.

Then there was only merciful silence.

"Thank goodness that's stopped," Joanne said to herself. But things had just gone from bad to worse. The copier had just died.

Patty looked at her with regret four hours later. "I don't know how to tell you this, Jo, but you got fired."

Joanne winced. "Well, I'd be lying if I said that surprised me. I'm sorry, Patty. Believe it or not, I truly thought I could handle that copier without a problem."

"I can't help but wish you were sure of that yesterday," Patty responded with a glare. "Temps Are Us is going to have to pay for the repair costs."

Joanne winced. "Really? Any idea about how much it's going to cost?"

Patty narrowed her eyes. "Thirty dollars an hour, to start with."

"I'll help with that. I still have some money in savings."

Patty lowered her head to her hands. "It's not just that, Joanne . . . it's my reputation that I need to worry about too."

"I'm sure I'll do better next time."

"Next time?"

"I bet this is just like falling off of a bicycle. I need to get right back on track. What do you have for me tomorrow?"

"Tomorrow?" Patty ran her fingers through her hair. "Don't you think you need a little break or something?"

"From what?"

"What about your foot?" her friend blurted.

"I'm fine, Patty. I went to see Dr. Sawyer. He said I'm great. I ready for anything, I promise."

"Well, all right," Patty said weakly as she glanced through the computer printout of job openings. "Ah. Here's one. All you do is work with people in this job. It's a job involving credit problems."

"What?"

"You call people who owe money to the Cullen Department Store and tell them that they need to pay."

"All right," Joanne said quickly. Calling people couldn't be that bad, could it?

"Joanne, I ought to warn you that these phone calls can be pretty tough . . ."

"I can be tough."

"And some people will probably hang up on you." Patty's eyes focused on Joanne's. "You'd have to call them back."

"I would. Please give me another try."

Patty closed her eyes for a moment and then opened them, looking horrified. "I don't know why I'm doing this—but I'll call Cullen's and tell them you'll be there tomorrow."

*   *   *

It turned out that credit collecting wasn't the job for her, either. As soon as she heard about her first client's troubles with Social Security, she told them they could have another month before anything more was done.

It wasn't any better with callers two or three, either. It was so hard to be tough with other people when she knew exactly how it felt to have financial troubles.

By noon, when Patty called her, Joanne was feeling frazzled but wasn't about to let her friend know that. "Things are just fine, Patty."

But something in her voice must have alerted her to the truth. "You sure?"

"Oh, yeah. It's great."

"How many calls have you made?"

"Um, four . . . but I was just about to start number five when you called."

"Don't you think you're going kind of slow?"

"These things take a while, Patty," she said evasively. "Did you know Mr. Rutherford was in a parachute squadron in World War II?"

"Who's Mr. Rutherford?"

"He lives in Montgomery. His grandson is really giving him some trouble lately. I wonder what's gotten into kids these days?"

There was a suspicious pause before her friend spoke. "I better let you get back to your calls. Uh, you haven't broken anything, have you?"

"No, as a matter of fact, I have not." Joanne hoped that she sounded as indignant as she felt. Honestly, did Patty have no faith in her at all?

"All right, then. But, listen, this is the only job I have for you this week."

Joanne was tempted to press her friend, but knew Patty well enough to lay off. "All right."

Five hours later, she left the office. She was worn out and emotionally drained. It was obvious, even to the people she was calling, that she wasn't suited for this job, either. Not eager to face questions about her day from her mother, she took the long way home. As she drove down the windy, tree-covered roads, she passed the Jackson house. She slowed her car to get a better look at the property.

An ugly orange and blue FOR SALE sign was posted in the yard. Next to it was another sign, announcing a town council meeting to discuss a zoning request on the land.

Making a sudden decision, Joanne parked the car and walked up to the house. She stepped carefully; the front yard was overgrown with weeds and crabgrass, and the front walkway was cracked and in disrepair. One of the gray shutters on the first floor hung crookedly and squeaked in a sudden gust of wind.

Joanne picked her way through the mess and peered in a window. The house looked washed-out in the bright light. "I wonder what you used to look like, when you were freshly painted and cared for," she murmured, then rubbed a circle on the window pane with an old tissue she found in her pocket. "Did slaves hide in your basement? Were you really an Underground Railroad station?"

Silence only met her musings.

Joanne stepped back and studied the peeling front door. All at once she began to imagine what the old house would look like fixed up, painted. A bright white would look pretty, maybe with black trim and a red door. The house was sprawling, but could look dignified and homey. And, if it had been an Underground Station, then it would need to be registered, too. And maybe whoever lived there wouldn't mind showing people the slaves' hiding place every once in a while. Maybe she should ask the ladies at the historical museum more about it . . .

"Hey, Jo," a voice called out.

She turned toward the sound. Mr. Jensen was standing on the other side of the street, watching her. "Hey," she answered, raising a hand. "Mr. Jensen, do you know much about this place?"

"Nope." He walked across the street and studied the sign posted in the yard. His lips pursed. "Only that it's probably not going to be here much longer."

"Really? Has someone bought it?" Disappointment coursed through her.

He shrugged. "I didn't hear that, but I did hear talk

of some people thinking this land might be a good place for a mini-mart."

Joanne felt the familiar pang of dismay. "But, this house has been here forever! That would be a real shame."

Mr. Jensen glanced at the house again, his eyes squinting in the sun. "I did hear that it was once a pretty important place."

Joanne turned to face the elderly man more fully. "Didn't this used to be an Underground Station?"

"Used to be a lot of things," he said cryptically. "Heard during Prohibition that there was quite a still in the basement."

"But about the Underground Station—"

"You know what the problem is these days, Joanne?" he interrupted.

He was obviously ready to tell her. "No sir."

"Ev'body's so busy these days. Too busy to do a little research about the history of our town." Mr. Jensen stepped forward, his left hand leaning on a cane, then eyed her meaningfully. "Too bad no one around here has the time or the smarts to learn a little bit about landmarks."

Joanne glanced at the sign casting shadows in the yard. "I guess that person would have to know where to look."

The lines in Mr. Jensen's face crinkled deeper as he barked with laughter. "Said like a young'n. I'd probably attend Bingo night on Wednesdays if I wanted some information 'bout things." He pulled out a worn handkerchief and coughed slightly. "The Landen Retirement Home has a weekly field trip there."

Obviously Mr. Jensen thought she had some time to spare. Of course, playing Bingo with retirees did sound more interesting than just looking forward to another part-time job.

"I've always wanted to play Bingo," Joanne said with a grin. "I'll have to think about that."

"Wouldn't think too long, Jo," Mr. Jensen said. He pointed to the sign. "Time's a-wasting."

"Thanks. I'll remember that."

As Joanne watched Mr. Jensen walk away, she glanced at the house again. A slate walkway led towards a back door. The remains of a shed or outbuilding crumbled in the yard. What had life been like in this house? Had there been a candle burning in the window to let escaped slaves know it was a safe haven? Perhaps there had been one of those cryptic quilts that hung on the railing instead? So many questions. She remembered hearing a story about how a doctor transported slaves under bales of hay in a wagon. Could that have been how they arrived?

However, no questions were to be answered right at that minute. She headed back to her car. As she pulled out, Joanne knew it was time to ask some questions about herself. How much did she care about that house? Enough to ask questions? Enough to get involved and concentrate on someone else's problems for a change?

There was a lot to think about. But maybe she especially needed to decide if she was ready for the answers.

Chapter Six

That Sunday she met Stratton at the coffee shop again. "Hey," she said as he walked in, clad in running shorts, an old white T-shirt, and worn shoes. He looked sexy and tan and impossibly handsome. She couldn't help but stare.

"Hey yourself," he grinned. "Sorry about the way I'm dressed. I couldn't wait to run this morning."

"That's no problem," Joanne forced herself to say casually, after taking in the way the worn cotton fabric defined the muscles in his chest and how cute his tan legs were. She forced herself to meet his gaze. "Um, did you go out last night?"

He pulled up a chair next to her and sat down. "Yeah. I drove to downtown Cincinnati last night."

The visions she had of him at one of the trendy bars

was not a good one. No doubt he had been the focus of many other girls' thoughts. Trying to keep her voice neutral, she said, "Oh, really?"

He nodded. "There's a guy I went through medical school with who lives downtown. He took me out."

Somehow she didn't like hearing that. "Wow," she said, instead of sharing her private thoughts. "That's great. Did you have a good time?"

"Sure. Got home too late, though."

She didn't need to hear that either. It was time to change the subject, fast. "Um, how's work?"

"Since it's the weekend, I'd say fine," Stratton answered, amused. "But I'd say the question would be better asked of you. Are you working tomorrow?"

"Yep. Well, I hope so, at least. It depends on what my friend Patty has available." She shifted in her seat uncomfortably. "I don't know how to tell you this, but my jobs haven't really been going too well."

"Is that right?"

She bit her lip and debated whether to risk telling him the whole, unvarnished truth or not. It was hard to admit to him that she was doing so badly. "I don't want to say too much, but actually, I've been kind of a disaster."

"What are you going to do?"

She relaxed as she realized that he didn't sound judgmental, only concerned. "Try harder, I guess. What else can I do? I'm used to working, being productive . . . I bet this next job will be better for me."

He looked concerned but said nothing.

Desperate to change the subject, Joanne asked, "Um, have you ever played Bingo?"

"Couple of times."

"Would you like to play with me on Wednesday night, if you're not too busy?"

Those blue eyes twinkled. "Gee, I don't think I've ever been asked out on a Bingo date before."

She could feel the familiar heat crawl up her neck again. "Well, I admit it's not as exciting as downtown Cincinnati, but I'd sure appreciate it."

Stratton reached out and covered her hand with his. "I was kidding. I'll be glad to go." He looked at her curiously. "Is this something new for you, or do you play often?"

Lord, please don't let him think she only played Bingo for fun. "Well, I'm going there actually to do a little investigative work."

A dark eyebrow raised. "Really? Tell me more. Now I'm really interested."

"Mr. Jensen—he's an old guy, you'll meet him soon—told me that a bunch of retired people play there on Wednesdays, and I need some information about that old Jackson House."

"The one you think was an Underground Station?"

She nodded. "I'm afraid that someone's going to get the building zone changed and tear it down, Stratton." She gazed at him, hoping that he could understand her feelings. "For some reason, it really bothers me. We can't just continue to plan for the future of the town by getting rid of the past."

"Maybe there is some way to compromise?"

"I don't know. For some reason, I get the feeling that someone wants to move quickly."

"Is there anything that you can do about it?"

She sighed. "Probably not, unless I can get some good information about the building's past. I read a little about the house at the library the other day, but not enough. I need to find some information that would make others care, too. Then, if I got some people on my side, maybe the town council would listen and not let anyone change the zone from residential to commercial."

Stratton seemed to consider her words. "Well, I'm game for playing Bingo and talking to people about it on Wednesday. It will be fun."

"Thanks. I really need you." She stumbled as she said the words and felt the familiar heat travel up her cheeks again.

"Is that right?"

Her hands twisted nervously together. "I mean . . . I really . . ."

Stratton squeezed her hand. "I know what you meant, Jo."

She stole another look at him, then, seeing only compassion in his gaze, relaxed her posture. Glancing at their hands clasped together, she mumbled, "Thanks."

"Don't worry about it. Everything will be fine."

"You sound so sure."

"Believe me, I've learned that sometimes a positive attitude is the only thing that can keep you going. The alternative is just too hard, you know?"

It seemed as if he knew exactly what she was feeling. She stretched her other hand out to meet their entwined ones. "I know."

They visited for another fifteen minutes and then parted ways. Joanne went home, prepared to help with some housework and look forward to another day of working at Temps Are Us.

Monday morning arrived with Joanne back in Patty's office. "So, how does this week look?"

"Gee, Jo . . ."

Joanne glanced at the calendar on the wall and groaned. Her mother had her monthly Payton Beautification Society meeting tomorrow. It was sure to be at least four hours long and involved getting shamed into joining committees. She had to get out of it. "Come on, Patty."

Patty glanced at the calendar and then back at the fax she was holding in her hand. "I can't believe I'm saying this, but something just came in that I think you could handle."

The words stung, but Joanne forced herself to think of her mother's committee meeting. Today they were going to plant window boxes for some buildings on Maine Street. She couldn't plant a daisy to keep alive for a week, much less the whole summer. Anything, even a small loss of pride was worth getting out of that project. "What job is it?" she asked dryly.

"There just happens to be a job opening as a receptionist at a vet clinic."

Fuzzy cute animals came to mind. None of them owing money. "Vet clinic? Whose?"

"Murphy's, down on Third. They just need someone to answer phones, greet people and their pets, and pull the files."

"Terrific. I can do that, no problem. Just as long as I won't be left alone with a machine."

"Ah, you're not allergic to dogs or cats, are you?"

"Patty, I'll be fine."

Her friend sighed. "I guess you're right. I should have known that you and Deb wouldn't mesh too well, anyway. And the collecting company was just a total mistake." She gave her friend a searching look. "I'll give you the paperwork and then you can go on over there."

As Joanne sat down and picked up a pen, Patty spoke. "Hey, I heard that you've been seeing a certain Doctor Sawyer around town."

Joanne beamed. "Yep. I've been introducing him to people. Lots of folks have been snubbing him in his office. They miss Doc."

"Well, Doc was there for thirty years," Patty pointed out.

"Change is a good thing."

"Spoken like someone who knows what she's talking about!"

Joanne grinned. "Speaking of which, I've got a date with a doctor tonight, and again on Wednesday."

Interest sparked in Patty's eyes. "Where are you going?"

"I think to the movies tonight, and to play Bingo on Wednesday."

"Bingo?"

"It's a long story, but suffice to say that I'm trying to find out some information about the old Jackson place."

"That old eyesore? All you need to know is that it's about to be removed from your line of vision."

Self-righteousness spurred Joanne on. "I can't believe you're saying that. It could be a very important landmark here in Payton."

Patty gave her a level look. "All that it is now is a fire hazard."

"Well, I'm trying to find out information about its past, to help save it. I'm pretty sure it was an Underground Station during the Civil War." Joanne's eyes widened as she realized that she meant every word. Suddenly, she was more eager than ever to prevent the destruction of the home.

"If you do save it, what are you going to do then?"

Plans began to fill her mind, but none cohesive enough to share. "I don't know. I haven't gotten that far."

"Well, you might want to soon. Your buddy Payton Chase wants to turn it into a mini-mart."

"What?"

"Yep. I heard that he's got his eye on the land."

Things had just gone from bad to worse. "You mean to tell me that it's *Payton* who wants to buy the land and tear the house down?"

"That's what I heard." Patty gathered some papers in a pile. "So, if you want to save it, you not only need to be thinking about why to save it . . . but how."

"Payton's got a whole lot more money than I do."

"That's true, but I'm not sure that everybody would agree that the property is best suited for a mini-mart. There might be a lot of people at that town meeting about zoning. You might have more people on your side than you think."

"I would hope so." Rapping her hand against Patty's desk, Joanne fumed. "Oh, this is just so hard. Don't people see that Payton isn't thinking about what's best for the town, he just wants to make money?"

Patty glanced at the office and then at her computer screen, where columns of numbers were shining back at her. "I hate to say it, but wanting to make money is not always a bad thing."

Joanne had to laugh. Her friend did have a point. "I know, but gosh . . . it's just so hard to think about that piece of the past getting torn down."

"I know. Joanne, if you need any help with that house, let me know. It's ugly, but I think you do have a point about trying to save it. I could at least give you some support in the community."

"Now, wait a minute, I never said . . ."

"And have a good time with that doctor," Patty continued as if she had never spoken. "If anyone needs some fun, it would be you, Joanne. You deserve a night out."

"Thanks."

Patty smiled. "No problem. But ah, Joanne?"

"Yeah?"

"Be careful at the vet clinic first, will you? I could sure use some good news at five o'clock today."

"You and me both, Patty, you and me both," Joanne said, then left, with a bounce to her step. For the first time in a month, she had plans to look forward to.

Chapter Seven

I *never want to own a pet*, Joanne privately decided as she attempted to comfort a distraught woman and her tiny, whiny, yipping dog. "It's going to be all right," she said ineffectually, her hand outstretched to comfort the pair.

"All right?" the woman shrieked.

The dog just growled.

Enough was enough. Joanne turned away and went back to her position behind the reception desk. After six hours, she had finally come to the conclusion that this was *not* a good job for her either. The noise was loud, the animals smelled, and several had really made a mess in the waiting room.

And then, there was that whole barking, growling, snapping thing. The noise was constant, and a head-

80

ache had become a permanent part of her body at least four hours ago. Now, she felt as if she talked in a staccato beat, to match the rhythm beating in her head.

Joanne surveyed the waiting room filled with pacing, anxious animals. The tension of the animals only seemed to bring out the worst in them, much like the atmosphere in a doctor's office did for her, she supposed. Well, at least it was almost time to call it a day. A substitute receptionist could only take so much.

She sat down and tried to look pleasant as another man and his cat entered the room. As she located the cat's file, she did have to admit that she was doing better at this job than the two previous ones. After all, it was already four o'clock and so far, nothing had gotten lost, everything still worked, and the worst thing she had to deal with was a really angry woman who didn't want to wait her turn in the waiting room: Puffy the Pomeranian had needed her shots, pronto.

But Joanne had diffused the situation with ease. It seemed the real problem was that Puffy's owner was having some serious marital issues with her husband. And Puffy, being the annoying yappy dog that he was, wasn't helping any.

Before she knew it, Joanne had found herself listening to the woman's marriage history and giving thoughtful advice. The woman vowed to put Puffy on a schedule and hand over half the chores to her husband. Joanne had even gotten a hug for her efforts.

It was a sign, and Joanne didn't like it. To her dismay, she seemed to be gifted in the receptionist-veterinarian field.

By five-fifteen, things were going so smoothly that she was mentally considering her choices of outfits for dinner. She needed something a little sexy, a little cute. Something that would convey her new attitude to Stratton, even if she wasn't quite sure what that attitude was. But then Nickel and Mrs. Edwards arrived and ruined her day.

Mrs. Edwards had been Joanne's sixth grade teacher. They had gotten along well enough, except for the small fact that Joanne had been more interested in Mike Shallahan that year instead of academics. Having already had five years of straight A's behind her, she had decided, by way of twelve-year-old logic, that it was time to let loose.

Mrs. Edwards had not been pleased when she realized that Joanne had decided that sixth grade was the perfect year to take a break.

Joanne turned in work late, barely studied for tests, and concentrated on Mike instead of the notes in social studies class. She had not lived up to her reputation, or that of the three siblings that Mrs. Edwards had taught before her, either. Because of that, Joanne had spent many afternoons in detention hall that year, which she had secretly thought a good thing because Mike was always there. Unfortunately, Mrs. Edwards had not felt the same.

Mrs. Edwards had not been happy with Mr. and

Mrs. Reece's lack of attention to Joanne's sixth grade year either. Of course, that had been the year that Jeremy had the chicken pox, Kevin had broken his arm, and Cameron had gotten in trouble for fighting. Joanne's fall from straight A's to B's had not caused much concern.

So Mrs. Edwards had taken it upon herself to push Joanne. Suddenly, Mrs. Edwards had been by her side at recess breaks, and study halls, encouraging, prodding. In spite of herself, Joanne began to look forward to the lady's attentions. The woman seemed to innately know that Joanne loved history and architecture, and did everything she could to promote those interests, even recommending Joanne for a district art history club. By February, she had developed a healthy respect for her teacher and told Mike Shallahan that she had no time for love. She immersed herself in her studies and the stories Mrs. Edwards told of the museums in Florence.

Now, as Joanne greeted the old teacher in the reception area, she felt the same uncomfortable thrill race up her spine again. She was still slightly afraid of Mrs. Edwards. Her beady blue eyes seemed to speak silent volumes, none of it good. Already she could imagine the speech that Mrs. Edwards was going to give her about not working to her potential. She squirmed when the elderly lady approached.

"Hello, Mrs. Edwards," Joanne welcomed her with a nod.

"Joanne," Mrs. Edwards answered, a knowing gleam in her eye. "How are you?"

"I'm fine, thank you," Joanne answered politely, then turned to a back counter and tried to keep herself occupied.

Luckily Mrs. Edwards didn't have to wait long to see the veterinarian. But things didn't look good. Nickel, the rabbit, was not healthy. Dr. Murphy thought it might have some kind of mouth infection.

While Dr. Murphy worked on Nickel, Joanne attempted to put the empty waiting room back in order. She hummed an old show tune while she picked up magazines and pet brochures that littered the floor. Next, she found the broom and dust pan and began to sweep the linoleum, hoping to remove the worst of the fur that littered it. Joanne had just made the first few swipes with the broom when she was startled by a yelp, followed by the appearance of Nickel, hopping down the hall.

"Joanne," Dr. Murphy called. "Can you find a way to stop Nickel?"

Nickel looked eager to remove himself from the premises. He had a wild look in his pink eyes, and his little nose was twitching to beat the band.

In spite of herself, Joanne felt sorry for the rabbit. She knew exactly how it felt to be frightened at the doctor's.

"Oh, poor Nickel," she cooed. "Here, bunny, let me help you." She scooped him up and cradled him close.

Nickel's fur was soft and warm. She stroked it lovingly.

But only got bit for her efforts.

"Ow!" she cried.

"Nickel?" Mrs. Edwards called out.

Joanne looked up to see Dr. Murphy and her former teacher approach her with concern. "Nickel bit my finger."

Quickly Dr. Murphy removed Nickel from her arms and passed him to Mrs. Edwards. "You all right, Jo?"

She stared at her finger. Two large chunks had been taken out of the tip. Blood gushed. Suddenly, the reality of what had just happened hit her full force. "Urrgh," Joanne said.

"Oh, no, I know that look. I think she's about to faint," Mrs. Edwards said dryly.

The veterinarian glanced at Joanne's coloring with some concern. "She's looking a little green to me. I don't think fainting is going to be Joanne's problem."

The words spun in the air around Joanne. She held her stomach with her one good hand. "Urrgh."

Dr. Murphy spoke calmly. "Joanne, go to the bathroom."

Joanne clasped her good hand in front of her mouth as she ran to the bathroom to lose her lunch. The door slammed shut after her.

Joanne gazed in the mirror after having emptied her stomach. Her skin was clammy, her eyes watered, and she had half a roll of toilet paper wrapped around one of her fingers. "I need to get out of here," she mumbled.

When she stepped out of the bathroom, Nickel and Mrs. Edwards were nowhere to be found and Dr. Murphy was leaning against the door to his office. "You going to be okay?"

What could she say? Joanne shrugged. "I think so."

"Sorry about that little accident. I've never seen Nickel so scared before."

"It's all right. Part of the job, I guess."

Dr. Murphy looked as if he was going to say more, but merely gestured to the door. "You better go down the street to Dr. Sawyer, Joanne. You might need stitches."

"Thanks," she said. Then, after grabbing her purse, she made her way down the street to Stratton's office. She reached the front door just as he was closing up. "Excuse me, Doctor, but could you take one more patient today?"

Stratton turned around, obviously to direct the person speaking to somewhere else, then paused when he noticed her. His eyes widened as he gazed at her pallid cheeks and bandaged hand. "Jo, what happened?"

Instantly Joanne realized just how glad she was to see him. Stratton looked comforting and warm, and his broad shoulders were exactly what she needed to lean on.

"I got mixed up with a snappy rabbit," she said, holding up her toilet-papered hand. Blood seeped through the paper, making it look like something out of an old horror movie.

His expression softened. "Come on in. Let's get you taken care of."

Joanne meekly followed him in, and concentrated on his back in front of her. Before she knew it, she was sitting on an examining table, Stratton had just washed his hands, and was unwrapping her hand.

"You sure wrapped this up pretty well, Jo," he said, glancing at the growing pile of tissue next to her.

Joanne realized she had probably used a whole roll for her one finger. "I wasn't really acting like myself," she said in defense. "The whole thing was so gross, I kind of got sick right after it happened."

He grinned. "I can imagine that experience must have been pretty traumatic, getting attacked by a rabbit and all," he said, trying to hide a smirk.

She ignored his attempt at humor. "It wasn't just any old rabbit, it was my former sixth grade teacher's!"

"Ouch," he said in sympathy. Then Stratton held her hand carefully, examining the torn skin from a few different angles. "That rabbit got you pretty good."

She gulped. "Do you think I need stitches?"

He shook his head. "I don't think so. It looks more like two puncture wounds. Let's just try to clean it well, butterfly it, then see what happens."

"Do I need a shot?"

He laughed. "Since we've already reviewed that

you've had a tetanus lately, I think we're all right there." Within a few minutes, Stratton finished, as good as his word. Her wound was cleaned, with antibiotic ointment applied, and bandaged.

She surveyed the results. "You are awfully capable, even without Mary."

"They try to encourage that in medical school."

"Thanks for doing this. I don't know what I would have done if I had come over here ten minutes later."

"You could have just called me. I think I would have made a special arrangement in your case."

Her ears perked up. "A special arrangement?"

Blue eyes sparkled. "Maybe I should be your doctor on call, twenty-four seven."

Her insides were melting from their playful banter. "That sounds like special treatment to me."

"You need it." He grinned, then laughed. "I tell you, Jo, it's a good thing the doctor's office is close to you."

His body felt warm, and she loved the way his hand felt in hers. Now that the danger of more shots was out of the way, the only thing that Joanne could think was that she couldn't wait to spend her evening with him, too.

"It is a good thing, Doctor," she murmured. "because I don't know when I'll need you next."

"There's no telling." His expression mirrored her own. "In your case, I might even have to begin making house calls." He leaned forward.

Joanne felt lightheaded, but this time because of Stratton. He smelled like soap and cologne; he smelled fresh and sexy. She ached for his touch. "I would look forward to your house calls."

His eyes darkened. "In the meantime, I'll just try to make you feel better."

Her chin raised, and his head bent lower. Joanne knew that she was about to receive her get-well kiss. But this one was different from their last. This kiss held promise of future kisses, embraces, and so much more. She reveled in the feel of his arms around her, pulling her towards him. He felt warm and solid and so very masculine.

When they did pull apart, Joanne looked at Stratton in surprise. "I feel better already," she said, then listened to the implications of her words. What was she doing? Did she really want him to stop? She forced a frown. "Well, almost," she corrected.

"Still not better?" he asked in mock surprise, then slid his arms around her and gathered her closer. "We can't have that. I guess I'll just have to try again."

Joanne snaked her arms around his shoulders. "Doctor, I think that's the least you could do."

Chapter Eight

"**I** know exactly what you're thinking about having a Bingo date, and let me just tell you right now that I don't want to hear it," Joanne said with a grin two days later as they entered the senior center and got in line for Bingo cards.

"I am not, and I have not, said a word about this," Stratton replied as he pulled out his wallet and paid the cashier for two cards and five games.

"But you were thinking it, I know it."

"But that does not incriminate me," Stratton countered.

As they entered the room, Joanne looked around. Long tables, lined edge to edge, circled the room. Many chairs were already filled. Already several people had their cards neatly lined up in front of them, the middle sections already punched out and ready to go.

"Where do you want to sit?"

Joanne looked around. "I don't know, somewhere near a lot of people." She scanned the area and then beamed as she noticed two empty chairs in the middle of the room. "I've got just the place, come on."

They snaked their way through the lines of tables. "Excuse me, sir, is anyone sitting here?"

An elderly gentleman in a rust-colored sweater peered over his glasses at them. "Nope."

Joanne looked at Stratton uncertainly, then turned back to the man. "Is it all right if we join you, then?"

"Sure. Don't see why not."

"Thanks." Joanne sat down, situated her purse next to her feet on the floor, and then waited expectantly. However, no one seemed inclined to offer a welcome. How was she going to find any information about the Jackson house if no one was especially chatty? Realizing that it was going to be up to her to start the conversation rolling, she spoke to the man again. After all, she wasn't at the senior center only to play Bingo. "This is our first time here."

"Humph."

She held out a hand. "My name's Joanne Reece. This is Dr. Stratton Smith. He's taken over for Doc. Have you met him yet?"

The man ignored her hand and peered at Stratton

through the corner of his eye. "Nope. Heard of him, though."

This was harder than she had thought. Joanne tried again to start a conversation. "What do you know about that old Jackson place, the one that's just come up for sale?"

The man wearily peered at Joanne again. "Not much. Just moved here last year."

"Well," Joanne hastened to explain, now that she had his attention, "I heard some rumors that it used to be an Underground Station during the Civil War, and was hoping that maybe someone here would know something about it."

The man's eyes narrowed. "I may be old, young lady, but I'm not *that* old."

"I didn't mean that you were in the Civil War!"

His eyes narrowed.

"I mean, I . . ." At his glare, panic edged her voice. "I just was hoping that someone . . ."

Just then an old lady in front of them turned around. "Who you need to speak with, dear, is Tilly."

Finally, some help. "Tilly?"

"Yes, dear. I believe she lived on that street some time ago. Just last Christmas I heard her telling some-one about it."

Joanne's shoulders relaxed. "Thanks, Mrs. . . ."

"I'm Mrs. Josie Hazelworth."

"Thanks Mrs. Hazelworth. I'm Joanne . . ."

"I know who you are, dear. I met your father some

time ago. He helped me with my will." She held up a hand just as Joanne was about to begin more introductions. "And I know who you are, too, Dr. Sawyer. I'd say the whole town has been a-buzzing about you."

Stratton held out a hand. "Pleased to meet you, Mrs. Hazelworth."

She nodded. "I don't think I'll be needing you anytime soon, but I imagine I'll be seeing you in the fall when the flu shots come in." She looked at him frankly. "You are still going to do those, now, aren't you?"

"Yes, ma'am."

"Dr. Whitman gave a senior discount."

"I'll do the same."

Mrs. Hazelworth glanced at the elderly man next to Joanne with a gleam in her eye. "Joanne, Tilly just arrived. She's sitting in the back row. She's in a wheelchair now. You'd have better luck sitting over next to her. Harry here takes this game pretty seriously. I wouldn't pester him any more."

"All right. Stratton, would you mind if we moved?"

"I've already picked up our cards," he said, then stood up. "Pleasure to meet you, Mrs. Hazelworth."

The spry lady nodded in satisfaction. "Likewise, I'm sure."

Joanne and Stratton then relocated to the back of the room, next to a lovely lady in a peacock blue sweater and gray slacks. "Tilly?" Joanne asked as they approached.

"That's me," the woman said as she glanced up from a series of five cards.

"I'm Joanne Reece, and this is Dr. Stratton Smith. Would you mind if we joined you? Mrs. Hazelworth just mentioned that you might be able to help me out with a couple of questions I have."

Tilly's faded blue eyes crinkled at the corners. "I'd be happy to, but at the break. We're about to start." She motioned to the middle-aged blond who had just approached the podium.

Joanne felt instant relief. Maybe this night would be productive, after all. "Okay."

After a few minutes of explaining the rules, the blond commenced to calling out letters and numbers. After the third one, Joanne realized that she was at a distinct disadvantage. Her mind kept wandering to what questions she wanted to ask Tilly, therefore delaying her search of each number called thirty seconds too late.

She glanced at Stratton. He seemed to be keeping up, but just barely. Tilly, on the other hand, was marking her cards with ease. Joanne had the sinking feeling that Tilly could have handled another five cards easily.

The next fifteen minutes weren't any better. Unfortunately, just as soon as she seemed to get the hang of each game, someone would call out "Bingo," and she'd have to start over again.

At the break, Joanne leaned back against her chair in exhaustion. Every muscle in her neck and shoulders seemed to have bunched up. She waved to Stratton when he got up to buy a lemonade from the booth at the back and seemed content to stay there and visit with the crowd.

"How's it going?" Joanne asked Tilly.

"Not well," Tilly replied grumpily. "Hate getting old. There was a time when I could handle double the cards. Now, with this darn arthritis, I'm lucky to be here at all."

"You sure seem like you're doing better than me, though."

Tilly looked at Joanne's card. Only about a third of the numbers from each game had been punched out. "That's not saying much."

"I guess you're right. But, ah, I actually came here hoping to talk with someone about the Jackson house. Mrs. Hazelworth said you might be able to help me with some questions."

"I might. I'm eighty-seven; I was born in 1913. My mom grew up with the people whose parents remembered when it was a station. There's lots of stories about that house."

"Is that right? It really was a station?"

"Sure. Fact is, there used to be a tunnel in their storm cellar that connected to another house on the street."

"Really? In that case, the station really was underground, hmm?"

Tilly smiled. "If I was you, and interested in the

history of the house, I would go down to the cellar and look around."

"I'll do that. I don't know why, but it really upsets me when I think about how that old house could just be torn down and forgotten."

"I know the feeling, dear."

Stratton arrived then, full of news about the people he met. Joanne smiled at his words. It seemed he had made not only some new friends in the room, but also some potential clients. At least their visit was going well for one of them.

The blond announcer began to call out numbers again. Despite concentrating on the numbers being called, Joanne still lagged behind. She was shocked when Stratton stood up and called out "Bingo!"

He stood up and then began to high-five everyone when the blond lady announced his prize of eighty dollars.

"Great going, Doc," one gentleman called out.

"Thanks," he called back and then sat down with a grin. "Joanne, hearing that guy call me 'Doc' made this visit all worthwhile," he murmured. "I'm glad you wanted to come here."

Joanne couldn't get over the fact that he was able to win a game while she could barely find the numbers. "Stratton, I can't believe you're so good at this!" she hissed.

"It's all in the wrist, Joanne," he joked when he

returned from claiming his money. "I'll take you out to dinner to celebrate."

"I'll look forward to that," Joanne said, then looked at her half-filled card in dismay. "I just can't believe you were able to find all those numbers so easily."

Tilly didn't look pleased with Stratton's good fortune either. "You'll learn that one day this will happen to you, Dr. Smith," she said, holding up gnarled fingers, "then it won't be so easy."

"You come on in to the office, Tilly, and I'll see what I can do for you."

Tilly glanced at the doctor with new respect. "Thank you, son. I just might do that."

Later, Joanne snuggled next to Stratton in the private booth at a local restaurant. "Thanks for coming with me to play Bingo."

"No problem, it was fun."

"What do you think about the news I heard from Tilly?"

"I think it would be worth your time to not only visit the house again, but to also get an appointment with the Payton Historical Society. If you're serious about saving the house, it's time to step up your involvement."

"I guess so." She snuggled closer, and was pleased when he placed his arm around her shoulders. "Stratton, what do you think about all of this?"

He brushed a kiss on her temple. "What do I think about what?"

She sat up to catch his expression. "About me trying to save a house, hunting for information, and trying to be a temporary worker. I'm a mess!"

"You're not a mess."

"That's no answer. Tell me what you think."

Stratton shifted uncomfortably. "I'm not sure if you want to know."

"What does that mean?"

"It's just that from my perspective, things seem a little different, that's all."

There was something in his tone that got her guard up. "Well, I think you ought to share your perspective with me."

He sighed. "All right," he began, his voice gentle yet serious. "Joanne, you're talking to someone who has never had the freedom to just play at working, or try out stuff. I've spent the last ten years of my life working like a dog to get here, get this practice in Payton. It seems to me that you're looking for things that are right in front of you."

"What is that supposed to mean?" She couldn't keep the hurt from her voice.

Stratton pulled his arm from her shoulder, then raked his fingers through his hair. "Look. I see a beautiful girl who has a family, a group of friends, and a whole community to fall back on. Yet, you're still not satisfied. You get upset because your parents want you to live with them until you find somewhere else that makes you happy. You complain about getting jobs that your friend Patty gets for you, when the truth is, I don't think you even have to work at all."

He paused for a moment and took a sip of water. Joanne stared at him in dismay and swallowed hard to hold back the tears that threatened. Then he continued. "And this whole thing about the Jackson house. You act like you care, but you haven't really tried to make a difference with it. When are you going to grow up and accept some responsibility, Joanne?"

What had happened? She couldn't believe that he was telling her these things. She thought he believed in her, that he was different from Payton. Hurt, she spoke sharply. "I don't have to sit here and take this, Stratton."

His tone matched hers. "You are exactly right. You don't have to. And I wouldn't be surprised if you stood right up and marched out of here."

She reddened as she realized that she had already grasped her handbag to do that very thing. "Stratton, you don't understand . . . I have been . . ."

He silenced her with a look. "I think I do. I think you're so afraid that you're going to fail again that you haven't been willing to commit to anything, even to me."

"You?"

"I'm running out of patience, Jo," Stratton said quietly, then sighed. "We're grown-ups, not in high school. I don't take girls out to dinner just to be friends. I don't kiss girls at night and not want anything more." He turned to her, his expression serious. "Let me be clear about this, so there's no misunderstandings between us. I want more from you than tours around town and introductions to prospective patients. I want a relationship and a future." His eyes narrowed. "But, Joanne, I want you to be ready for that, too."

Reluctantly, she admitted to herself that there was some truth to what he was saying. Even though they made sense, they scared her half to death. *Had* she been taking Stratton for granted? Her future, her privileges for granted? At a loss for words, she hedged. "I don't know what to say."

Stratton held out a hand and skimmed a finger down her cheek. The gesture softened his words but didn't make them any easier to hear. "Maybe that you're going to finally sit down and do some thinking about what you want to do with your life, Joanne."

"But—"

He met her gaze, openly and honestly, and cut her excuses off. "It's time to stop running, and start planning."

Her heart pounded at his ultimatum. "But I'm not ready to do that."

Stratton folded his arms across his chest. "Then I guess we don't have anything more to say right now."

Then Joanne did something she didn't think she had

the nerve to do. She stood up, grabbed her purse, and left the restaurant. She didn't look back once.

Not even when Stratton didn't call out to ask her to stay.

Chapter Nine

Her heart sinking, Joanne left Stratton and went straight to the one place where she knew she could find comfort: home.

In her heart, Joanne knew Stratton was right about so many things. She had only been going through the motions with her life. It was time to grow up and be honest with herself. But knowing that didn't make it easier.

When she arrived home she wandered into the living room and slumped on the couch. She bit her lip to stop the tears that threatened to fall.

"Joanne?"

She looked up to meet the eyes of her brother Kevin. "Hey," she said.

Kevin walked in, followed by her two other brothers, Jeremy and Cameron, as well as her parents. "What's going on? Didn't you hear us in the kitchen?"

She shook her head. "No, I'm sorry."

Ever the gentleman, Kevin eyed her expression, then sat down and enfolded her in his arms. "What's wrong, Jo?"

She buried her face in her older brother's shoulder. "Nothing. Everything."

"You want to talk about it?"

"It's not gonna help."

Kevin glanced at the others in the room, then shrugged and continued. "Does it have to do with that doctor guy you've been seeing?"

"No, yes, oh, I don't know anymore," she mumbled into his chest. "Everything in my life is such a mess, Kevin. And I think Stratton's sick of me."

Kevin raised his head again to glance at the rest of the family. All looked confused by Joanne's words. His mother motioned for him to pull away so she could speak.

Joanne sniffed a few times, then finally brought herself to look at her family. Everyone regarded her with curiosity. She began to feel even more uncomfortable—which she hadn't known could be possible. "What are all of you guys doing here?"

"Getting ready to have dinner," Daphne answered. "You've already eaten though, right?"

Tears welled in her eyes again. "We were, but Stratton got mad at me. I left the restaurant."

Cameron winced. "Uh-oh. What did you do, Jo?"

Joanne sat up straighter. "You know Cameron, I'm sure there are other people in this world who wouldn't immediately think the problem was with his sister. What about Stratton?" she asked with a whine. "How come you aren't offering to go beat him up or something?"

Her three brothers exchanged glances, then looked at her dad. Jim shrugged his shoulders in a resigned way.

"Do you want me to, Jo?" Jeremy said.

Jim Reece sighed. "Now, Joanne. I've spoken with Stratton several times now. I like him. You two will patch things up in no time. He's a great doctor."

"So," Joanne said defensively. "What difference does that make?"

"Hey, he did fix your nasty-looking foot," Cameron supplied.

"Cam—"

Daphne entered the conversation. "Joanne, dear, your father told me that the two of you were going to play Bingo at the senior center to find some information about the Jackson house," she said smoothly. "Did you go there?"

"Yes. Stratton even won a game. And I met an old lady who told me some stories about the house."

"Is that why you're mad, because he won a game and you didn't?" Kevin said.

Joanne's hand itched to slap him. Why did older

brothers always consider their younger sisters to be terminally fourteen? "No, Kevin! I got mad at him because he insinuated that I was afraid of my future. I think he even hinted that I was ungrateful for all of you."

Cameron jumped right in, seeming to only be focused on their history of game-playing. "Jo, don't you remember that time when we played Life and you swore that Denise cheated?"

"She did! You just didn't see it!"

"You weren't happy about it though," Kevin said.

"I remember that I had to be on Denise's team, and you said . . ." Jeremy began.

Joanne glared at her little brother. "You were twelve at the time. Nothing you remember counts."

"Stop!" Daphne called out. "How come when each of you is alone with me, you are kind, rational adults, but when you're together, you all turn twelve again?"

Cameron grinned. "Old habits die hard."

Daphne held up a hand when it looked as if another set of bickering was about to begin again. "Joanne, please just tell us about what happened tonight."

"All right. Tilly, the old lady, shared some information. Then, Stratton and I went out to dinner, and he said that I ought to seriously pursue my goal of saving the house. Did you all know that it's Payton who wants to change the zoning and put in a mini-mart?"

"Figures," Cameron said.

Joanne nodded in indignation. "I told him that I had been trying to save the house, well, kind of. He said, no, I had just been playing around with it. He thought I ought to go to the Historical Society tomorrow and actually tell them that I, Joanne Reece, want to be in charge of saving the Jackson house!" She looked around the room and waited for the snide remarks to begin.

But they only looked interested. "And . . ." Kevin prodded.

"Guys, you don't understand. No one's going to listen to me! I'm the town flake! I completely messed up at the vet hospital, not to mention at the copy room at Envirovision."

"What does that have to do with saving the house?" her mother asked reasonably.

"Stratton's onto something there," Jim said. "You ought to do those things. I think that's a great idea, Joanne."

Tears of frustration burned her eyes. "Come on, Dad, my shop burned down! I'm working as a part-time temporary worker. I'm the laughingstock of the community! No one would take me seriously."

"The shop burned down because of an outdated wiring problem, Jo. Nobody ever thought it was your fault," her father pointed out.

"And even I could have told you that you're not cut out to be a temp. You have never done well with other people's rules," Cameron said.

"But—" Joanne tried to interject.

Kevin cut her off. "I don't know why you think of yourself as a klutz, anyway. You've only had a few minor mishaps."

"Everyone in this town likes you, Joanne," Cameron stated. "I happen to think you would do a great job returning that house to its former glory."

"You could even use your insurance money to make it livable for yourself," Jim added.

"That would be a great idea. You could live in the upstairs, and turn the back room and cellar into a kind of museum," her mother finished in that practical way of hers.

"But—"

Cam sat on the edge of the couch. "I'll have a few weeks off after my court case, Jo; I'll help you get started."

"But—"

"Now, as far as Stratton goes . . ."

"Why are you so upset with him?" Kevin unwrapped his arm from her shoulder.

"He wants me to get serious about our relationship. He says that I'm holding back, that I'm afraid to trust him."

"And?" Daphne stood up to straighten the crease in her slacks.

She looked at her family. "And, well, after Payton, and everything, I think I have every right to be."

"And that's when you left," Jim clarified.

"Yes."

Kevin nodded. "*Now* I understand why you're so upset."

Finally, someone who understood. "Thanks," Joanne said with a smile.

Kevin grinned. "You really blew it, didn't you?"

"No! There's no way—"

Her father cut her off. "I'm starving. Daphne, you think we can go ahead and eat?"

Daphne looked at her daughter with a touch of sadness. "Of course. Everything's ready. Joanne, come on in here and join us. We're having chicken salad and fruit."

"No thanks."

For the first time in Joanne's life, her mother didn't try to interfere. "Well then, let's go eat before your father grumbles any more." Daphne then stood up and led the way to the kitchen.

"I'm allowed to grumble, it's been a heck of a day," Jim pointed out as he made his way into the kitchen.

Joanne watched them all leave, one by one, except for her brother Cameron. Although she was fond of each of her siblings, she was closest to Cam, perhaps because they were only eleven months apart in age.

Cameron knelt in front of her, so they were eye to eye. "I never told you this, Jo, but I think you're too hard on yourself. You don't have to be perfect; nobody expects it of you."

"I don't expect it either."

"No, but you have a way of forgetting that *everyone* has obstacles in their lives. Everyone trips and falls at one time or another. I, for one, am glad of it. I happen to think those obstacles are there for a reason, to make life more interesting." He looked away for a moment, then back at her. "Do you remember last year, when I was hunting for that treasure, and I was going to take a job in Chicago?"

"How could I ever forget?" Joanne smiled. "It was one of the most memorable things that's ever happened to our family, not to mention that you met Mary Beth that way."

"If she wasn't out with her girlfriend Julie right now, she'd be glad to hear that," he teased. Then Cam ran a hand through his dark blond hair. "But do you recall that I didn't feel that way at first? I felt like an idiot, searching for something I wasn't even sure existed. And I was worried about telling Mom and Dad, sure they were going to tell me to grow up."

"They did just the opposite! They embraced the whole treasure hunt with open arms."

Her brother nodded. "Looking back, it was the best thing that ever happened to me. So was meeting and marrying Mary Beth."

"But, Cameron, this is different."

"How so?"

"What if I fail? You, at least had a law degree and a future in Chicago to fall back on."

"It wasn't the right future for me, Joanne. And you won't know if you've failed until you've tried."

She remembered telling him almost those exact words of advice not so long ago. "I wish it were that easy."

"Come on, Joanne. You know the answer to that." He grinned. "Nothing worth having is easy to attain."

Joanne smiled. How many times had they heard their father say those same words? "What about Stratton?"

"Who says you have to decide about your future with him today, or even this week? If it's meant to be, it will happen. Why don't you just enjoy being with him, instead of that jerk Payton?"

Suddenly her world felt much clearer. She stood up and walked with her brother to the kitchen. "You didn't like Payton too much, did you?"

"Suffice it to say that if you had ever gotten really serious about him, I may have had to resort to physical harm."

"For him or me?"

He grinned. "Wouldn't have mattered; I would have happily maimed whoever was closest."

As they walked into the kitchen, Cameron threw an arm around her shoulders. "Keep your chin up, Jo. Everything will be all right. And I'll let you in on a secret: this town of ours is a pretty good place to live. The people will support you."

*   *   *

When the phone rang that night, Stratton picked it up with trepidation. His only calls at one in the morning were emergencies, and he was in no hurry to get out of bed.

"Dr. Stratton Sawyer," he muttered into the phone, already searching for a pair of khakis on the floor to pull on.

"Stratton? Are you all right?" Joanne said hesitantly.

He sat back down on the edge of the bed. "Hey. Sorry. Usually the only calls I get this late are for work."

"Oh, I hope I didn't bother you."

Joanne's voice sounded hesitant, contrite. "No, it's no bother."

"Listen, the reason I'm calling is to apologize. There was no reason for me to be so snippy with you tonight."

"You're entitled to your own opinion, Joanne."

"That's true, but not to express myself in that way. And I should have never left you in that restaurant. No one deserves that kind of behavior. I'm sorry about everything. I guess I've just been a little on edge."

Immediately he felt the same pull toward her that he always did. "It's understandable."

There was a pause on the line. Stratton waited, wondering what she would say next.

"I was hoping I could make it up to you by taking

you out tomorrow night. I've got some things I want to say in person."

Did he really want to subject himself to that kind of embarrassment again? To ask her to choose him or nothing, and risk her choosing the latter? "Actually, Joanne—"

Her words cut him off. "Because I realize that I was wrong about us."

His eyes widened and he leaned back in bed. She was full of surprises tonight. "Oh, really?"

"I'm not saying that we need to go get married or anything, but ah, I think that there's definitely something between us, just like you said. I want to find out what it is."

The "definitely something" was truly an understatement. "I would agree with that," he said softly, curious about what other revelations she was about to spring.

"And I was thinking that we have something that is probably worth exploring."

"Probably." He couldn't hide the smile in his voice.

"So, ah, tomorrow night?"

"When do you want to meet? My office hours end at six on Wednesdays."

"I'm going to go over and talk to the people at the historical society around four tomorrow. How about I walk over when I'm finished with that?"

"That will be great, I'll look forward to it."

"Really?"

Stratton could sense her pleasure. He wished she was nearby so he could give her a hug. "Really, Jo."

"Maybe we could go for a walk or something?"

"Sure, whatever you want."

"Or to the movies . . . we could go to the movies."

He chuckled. "We'll find something to do, I'm sure of it."

"Oh great. I feel so much better now. I'm so glad that I called you," she added, speaking in that cute way that she did when she got excited. Stratton listened with pleasure for a moment, then glanced at the clock and knew it was time to get off the phone.

"Jo, I'm sorry, but I've got to get some sleep now," he said, yawning.

"Oh, okay," she replied. "You know, all of a sudden, I'm exhausted, too. Good night, Stratton."

" 'Night." He hung up the phone, and then lay back down again, this time with a bemused smile. What was up with Joanne Reece? he thought, as he arranged the covers over himself. Something must have happened to her to make her change her mind about the two of them in just a few hours.

He, for one, couldn't wait to find out what it was.

Chapter Ten

There was utter chaos at the Historical Society. Joanne stood at the door and didn't know whether to laugh or cry. A group of twenty-five first graders were wandering around, being told not to touch anything. It looked like there was about to be a mutiny at any minute.

Another group, this one composed of middle-aged women, was sitting in the partitioned formal living room. They looked irritated and peeved.

The lone clerk seemed as though she was about to burst into tears at any minute. Joanne remembered her from an earlier visit. "Hi, Missy. Is Mrs. Abrams available? I called earlier today and left a message on the answering machine."

Missy's expression became pained. She crooked a

finger at Joanne to lean closer. "She's not here," she whispered.

"Oh. Well, when will she get back? It's kind of important that I speak with her."

Missy shook her head. "No, I mean that she won't be in for a while. She broke her leg two days ago on the bike trail."

"Oh my gosh! I hope she's going to be okay."

"I think she will, but she's going to be home for quite a while. But in the meantime, all kinds of things need to be done and no one knows what to do."

Joanne didn't know what to say. "Wow."

Missy nodded in understanding. "I know. Everything is a mess. We need to find someone to take over for the next six months. Mrs. Abrams is going to have to have surgery and then physical therapy." She gestured to a group of ladies sitting at an old table, each with a stack of papers in front of them and all wearing pained expressions. "Those ladies are part of the Board of Trustees over there. They've been trying all morning to decide what to do, but I don't think they're having much luck."

Joanne glanced at the women. One of them was writing notes in a spiral notebook, another was pointing to a large calendar that hung on a cart. All looked pretty weary and disgruntled. "They do look like they're having a tough time."

"I hope they come up with some ideas quick," Missy exclaimed. "In the meantime, classes keep coming for tours, and people keep coming into the building for records!" She sighed. "There were three messages waiting for me this morning, two from volunteers needing to change their schedules, and another from a guy in Tennessee who wants information about his great grandmother." Missy pointed to her own note-book and stack of papers then pulled a lock of hair behind an ear. "I'm the only one working, and I've never done it all by myself! I don't know what to do! It's a nightmare."

Joanne glanced at the first graders. Several had re-sorted to playing with the antique kitchen display. "Uh-oh."

Missy nodded. "Uh-oh is right." Just then one little boy decided to try to climb into an old laundry tub. "Oh, Lord. I better go take these little guys around or their teachers are going to go bald from pulling their hair out!"

"Good idea. I know a couple of those ladies. I'll go see what's going on. Hey, do you think they'll make you the interim director of this place now, Missy?"

"Gosh, I hope not; I don't want the position. I've only been working here a little over a year. I'm fine with helping out, and giving tours, but I am not pre-pared to be director, even for a little bit. I don't have any educational background for this." She gestured toward the computer, the bookshelf full of reference texts, and the group of students, and sighed. "I mean,

I like working here and everything, but I've got a lot to learn."

Joanne felt a pang of sympathy for the younger woman. She knew exactly how it felt to be overwhelmed. "You hang in there, okay? Let me know if I can do anything to help."

"Thanks," Missy replied, then pasted a smile on her face and went to face the first graders.

Seeing that her arrival had been noticed by the ladies, Joanne straightened her dress and went to say hello to them. It was amazing that her mother wasn't a part of this group, since she seemed to have her hand in most of the committees in town.

However, she did recognize Mrs. April Peterson and Ms. Barbara Kelly. The ladies looked toward her in relief when she stopped in front of them.

"Hi, Mrs. Peterson," Joanne said with a smile. "How are you? Missy told me about what happened with Lori Abrams."

The elder lady gestured toward a vacant chair for Joanne. "Can you believe that? I'm astounded!"

"What happened, exactly?"

"I'm not exactly sure, but I heard it was just some kind of freak accident involving her bike and two other bike riders. I think they were trying to move to the right for a jogger or some such thing." Mrs. Peterson closed her eyes briefly. "I just feel so sorry for her. What a terrible thing for her to be going through." The other ladies nodded in agreement.

"Missy said that y'all don't expect Mrs. Abrams back for a while."

Another lady answered. "Not for at least six months. I believe she's planning to go to Arizona to be with her sister to recuperate after surgery." She shook her head. "And, unfortunately, this accident couldn't have come at a worse time. Lori had meetings scheduled all this week, as well as an artist reception. She is just so integral to everything that goes on here. The volunteers love her. I just don't know how we're going to manage."

"Um, any idea who you're going to get to fill in?"

"None whatsoever."

"We'll need to hire an interim director as soon as possible. We were just looking at our list of volunteers to see if we thought any of them might be interested," Mrs. Peterson said, glancing at the list of names in front of her. "Barbara? Do you think Audrey might be available?"

A red-headed lady answered. "Gosh, I don't think so. I heard she was pretty busy with her work at the library."

Joanne listened to the conversation with dismay. "That's too bad this happened. I feel bad for Mrs. Abrams, but I sure needed some help locating records about the Jackson place."

"What exactly are you looking for, Joanne?" Mrs. Peterson asked.

"Well, I'm interested in the history of the Jackson

place, especially its involvement in the Underground Railroad."

"Any idea how you would go about finding that information?" Mrs. Peterson asked.

Joanne nodded at the question. "Well, yes, as a matter of fact. I thought I'd investigate the tax records, and I've already begun to record some of the town members' oral histories of the house." Joanne sighed. "I had hoped to use the Society's resources to investigate further, perhaps even draw up a case to present to the town council when they meet next week. I can't believe Mrs. Abrams is gone. I was really hoping for the Society's help. Now I don't know what I'm going to do."

Barbara Kelly leaned forward with interest. "Is that right? You already know how to go about doing all of that?"

Joanne nodded. "Sure. After all, my degrees are in history and fine arts. I did my master's thesis on the history of Depression-era glass."

Several of the ladies looked at each other. One leaned over and spoke with Mrs. Peterson in a whisper. Mrs. Peterson spoke then, her red lips curved at the edges. "Forgive me if I'm mistaken, but didn't your shop burn down recently?"

Joanne nodded. "Yes."

"And aren't you working as a temp for Patty Austin?"

"Yes," she said cautiously, not sure of the direction

of this conversation. "But, uh, I've been only working as a temp temporarily."

Another lady spoke up. "Seems like such a waste of your talents, Joanne. After all, for a woman of your exceptional skills, to be working by the hour," she asked.

Joanne shifted uncomfortably. "It's not too bad. I was just doing that until I decided what I wanted to do next."

"Joanne, your mother said you earned quite a few honors in school," Barbara said. "Didn't you graduate *summa cum laude* in college?"

"Yes," Joanne said again, this time more hesitantly. Why were these women so interested in her credentials all of a sudden?

Mrs. Peterson tapped a mauve nail against the table. Her diamond ring glinted in the light. "All of that learning. All of those years of college, all of that hard, hard work." She sighed. "It would be a shame not to put it to good use, Joanne."

Hadn't she just said she was trying to figure out her future? It was one thing to defend herself to her parents. It was quite another to defend herself to her mother's cronies. It was definitely time to leave. Joanne began to sit up. "Well, I think I'll just . . ."

"I think you would be terrific as our temporary director, Joanne," Mrs. Peterson said boldly.

Joanne sat back down. "Excuse me?"

"I think you would be just the person we need to

take over for a while. You appreciate Payton, and our town's history, to boot."

"Well, I, ah—"

Ms. Kelly leaned forward. "Don't you think that this would be just the thing to help you get situated?"

Joanne looked helplessly at the women.

"Barbara, dear, she's dating Dr. Sawyer," another woman pointed out.

"And this building is just blocks from his office," Mrs. Peterson said, a pleased smile on her face. "And just think how much backing you would have from us in your quest to save and then refurbish the Jackson home . . ."

"If you were Payton's Historical Society Interim Director," Barbara finished.

"You could even start right away."

The comments were throwing Joanne for a loop. "But, ah—"

"Barbara, what was Lori's salary again?"

Barbara looked in her notebook and then announced a figure. It was an amount that made Joanne's heart palpitate. In fact, it was more than the profit she made from her antique shop. A lot more, if Joanne considered how she wouldn't have the long hours or overhead.

Joanne tried to keep her voice even. "Is that what the board would be offering me?"

Several of the ladies exchanged looks. Just then a loud crash was heard, followed by a deafening scream.

Obviously one of the first graders had gone somewhere he or she wasn't supposed to.

Mrs. Peterson coughed discreetly. "Actually, that
would be the salary, Joanne, without the signing bonus."

"Signing bonus?" Both Joanne and two of the
women said at the same time.

Mrs. Pennington glanced at the door, saw Missy
frantically waving toward them, and turned back to
Joanne. "That's the bonus we customarily give people
who agree to take the job *immediately*." Mrs. Peterson
wrote an amount on a blank page on the spiral note-
book. "I have a feeling that a signing bonus could go
a long way when someone is trying to get her life back
together, Joanne," she hinted.

Joanne looked at the figure, then around the room.
Suddenly, her life felt as if there were a thousand op-
portunities waiting for her. Did she really need to consider it? She glanced at the doorway. The first graders
were filing out the door. One of the teachers seemed
to be giving Missy a piece of her mind. Missy glanced
at the ladies plaintively.

Joanne met the gaze of the women who were all
staring at her. She knew what they were trying to do;
they needed someone as soon as possible, and were
trying to railroad her into agreeing to the job so they
wouldn't have to go through the pain and aggravation
of advertising, interviewing, and hiring someone new.

They were trying to bribe her with money to get her to do that.

But that was all right. There had to be a reason that she had arrived in the middle of all of the chaos. She'd take the money, and the job, and deal with the consequences later.

Her mind made up, Joanne stood up and faced the women. "Ladies, I accept. I'm pleased to take the job."

"Oh, thank heavens," Barbara exclaimed. "Missy told me that there's another tour due to arrive in one hour."

"This one is kindergarteners!"

Joanne sat back down. What had she just gotten herself into?

Chapter Eleven

Stratton waved goodbye to the young mother and her two-year-old as they left his office. He had had a good day. No one had come and immediately left after realizing that Doc wasn't in, and he was developing a fragile relationship with Mrs. McCluskey.

Wearily he wandered to his office and looked at the stack of files that now needed to be written in and checked. He hoped he could finish his work quickly so there would be time to go home, get cleaned up, and prepare for his date with Joanne.

For what seemed to be the hundredth time that day he thought about her late-night phone call, and the implications that her words had. Had she been serious about her promises? Was she ready for a commitment?

He tapped a pencil against a file. For that matter, was he ready? He honestly didn't know.

He could admit that he smiled whenever he thought of her, though. What was it about her that attracted him so much? Of course she was beautiful. Any woman with almond-shaped gray eyes and had auburn hair that fell to her waist would be. But there was more to his attraction than that. Maybe it was that he had never been around anyone so perky before. Maybe it was her lovely smile that she shared with everyone. Honestly, it was like she had an angel on her shoulder. He found her enthusiasm thrilling.

Stratton had made his way through four files when Mrs. McCluskey appeared, looking the opposite of Joanne Reece—worn out and disgruntled. "Mr. Reece is here."

"Really? Why?"

Her lips thinned. "It seems he had a little accident. Looks like he might need a stitch or two. I sent him on back to Room Three. And I'm going on home, now."

Stratton had no reply to that. Of course Mrs. Mac would be leaving, it was six-thirty on the dot. "Thanks. I'll be right there."

He knew there was no use in asking her to stop by Mr. Reece's room to tell him that the doctor would be right in. According to Mrs. Mac's job description, her day was over.

When Stratton entered the room, Jim Reece was sitting on the table, thumbing through a *Golf Digest* with one hand and holding the other, wrapped in what looked to be an old T-shirt, straight up like a flag.

"Hi, Jim."

"Hi there, Stratton. Maybe you could help me out a little here. Cut myself while slicing a bagel."

Stratton winced. "I've seen those injuries before. They sting pretty bad."

"Daphne said she heard it is one of the most common injuries in the kitchen."

Stratton washed his hands, slipped on gloves, and then began to slowly unwrap Jim's hand. He smiled as he recalled how Joanne had wrapped her finger in a similar way. Then, he focused his attention on Jim's cut. A one-inch gash occupied the lower portion of his thumb. "It's good you came in. You're going to need a few stitches."

Jim nodded. "Figured as much. Told Daphne not to hold dinner for me." He paused for a moment, lips pursed as he looked at the gash. "They've got those bagel-cutting contraptions out now in stores. Daphne showed me one once. Plastic things, where you stuff the bread into the middle and then slice where the arrows tell you to. Make you feel like you're in grade school again, needing directions for everything."

"Sounds handy."

"I told her the thing was a waste of money. But now I'm thinking, maybe not." Jim glanced at the slash with a grimace. "This is going to ruin my golf game on Saturday."

"Probably," Stratton agreed as he cleaned the wound, then numbed the area with an injection. "This shouldn't take too long to sew up. You might even make dinner after all."

"Hope so." Jim continued his dialogue. "Maybe it was the knife. I don't know when Daphne sharpened it last. I heard something about dull knives causing accidents when cutting tomatoes. Have you heard that?"

Stratton opened his mouth to reply but was cut off again.

"Too many accidents with knives these days," Jim groused. "Turned the kitchen into a dangerous place." Jim glanced at his hand, then continued speaking. "By the way, I called Joanne on her cellphone and told her just to meet you here for your date."

Stratton paused. "That was thoughtful of you."

"She thinks the world of you, which is good. Never did like that Payton myself."

Stratton figured this was as good a time as any to get some information about Joanne's love life. "I heard he broke up with her when her shop burned down."

"Dropped her like a hot potato," Jim said with disdain. "Creep."

"I saw him at your club the other night, and around town a few times. I guess he's pretty well known?"

Jim gave Stratton a measured glance. "You could

say that," he said, his expression conveying much more than his words. " 'Course, you could also say that he's an idiot." Jim paused for a moment, then directed his attention back to Stratton. "Glad you're not."

Stratton smiled at the quasi-compliment. "Thanks. Joanne's volunteered to help me out a little now—to introduce me to some people, show me around town."

Jim coughed slightly as he watched the needle pierce his skin. "I heard something different from Joanne the other night. Thought you two were a little more serious about each other." He raised an eyebrow. "Seems to me, you don't need much of a tour guide in this town, if that's what you're looking for."

Stratton grinned. "Actually, that isn't what I'm looking for, but Joanne seemed comfortable with that arrangement. However, I think we're getting past that."

"She is a skittish little thing. Always had more book sense than anything. The other four, I always knew they could take care of themselves. But Jo, she's always had her heart on her sleeve." Jim met the doctor's gaze. "And that's not always a good thing."

"No sir."

"She can get hurt that way. Everyone has tried to look out for her, even her brother Jeremy, and he's four years younger."

"Does he live here, too?"

"No. He's up in Columbus now. Just finished his junior year. One more year of college to pay for."

"You've put all five through?"

"I've tried to—we're not done with Jeremy yet. That's what money's for, son, in my opinion. To spend on your children." He waved a hand distractedly. Stratton stopped his work until Jim was still again. "And they've certainly come up with ways to spend it."

Thinking of his own circumstances, he only said, "I imagine so."

"But next year, Daphne and I are going to China."

Stratton took another stitch. "China. Is that right?"

"Yep. Going to walk on the Great Wall."

Stratton knotted off the thread, then stopped to admire his handiwork. "Now, that will be something to look forward to."

"Yep. That's the secret, son. Anticipation." He drew out the word, making the five syllables seem like ten.

Just then, the door opened and Joanne appeared, as if on cue. "Anticipation," Stratton repeated. "I'll be sure to remember that."

"Anticipation?" Joanne echoed, as she entered the room. "What are you two talking about?"

"College, kitchen gadgets, your dad's golf game, and, ah, China," Stratton said.

"Wow, I'm sorry I missed it." She walked farther into the room and absently kissed her father on the head. "How are you doing, Dad? Mom told me you had a little accident."

Jim looked down at his thumb and scowled. "I've been better, but I'll be fine soon. Your doctor here is doing a good job."

Joanne blushed. "Dad."

Jim ignored her. "Where are you two going tonight?"

"Actually, we have a little celebrating to do," she said, standing a little straighter. "You're looking at the new interim director of the Payton Historical Society."

Both men stared at her in shock.

"Say again?" Jim said.

"It's a long story, but suffice it to say that I was in the right place at the right time. Poor Mrs. Abrams broke her leg and is going to be in traction for quite a while. They needed someone with experience, and I needed a job that didn't involve animals, collating, or bill collecting."

Her father's eyebrows rose at the explanation. "Those kinds of jobs are hard to come by."

Stratton cut to the chase. "Are you happy with this? I thought you were going to take some time off. Is this the job you want?"

Joanne stared at Stratton. That really was the question, wasn't it? Then the feeling came over her, the same feeling that she had felt when she had signed the lease on her antique shop. It was the right job, and more importantly, it was the right job for this time in her life. She was finally coming to terms that she couldn't base her future on past dreams. Then, realizing that she had been staring at Stratton without voicing any of these things, she spoke. "Yes, I'm happy. I think everything's going to be okay."

Stratton glanced at her, puzzled. "I'm glad."

Then she finally paid attention to what Stratton and her dad were doing and paled. A criss-cross pattern of black stitches marked his thumb. A bloody rag sat forgotten on a table. The room began to tilt. "I think I'll explain to you what happened when you guys are all done," she said weakly.

"There she goes," Jim muttered.

"Just a sec," Stratton said to his patient, then immediately walked over and guided Joanne out of the room. Once they were in the hall, he deposited her in a chair, and pressed her head to her knees. "You sit tight, okay, sweetheart? We're almost done."

The endearment rang in her ears. Then the room spun a little. Joanne clasped her hands to either side of the seat. "That sounds like a fine idea, Doctor," she said without argument.

Minutes later, Stratton and her father met her in the hall. Jim looked sporty with a bandaged hand and a calculated smile. "I'm going to go on home to your mother, Jo," he said, already fishing in his gray slacks for his keys. "I'm guaranteed to get a steak dinner instead of that casserole out of this mishap. Daphne might even let me eat it in the living room while I'm at it."

Joanne laughed, knowing her dad was correct. If anyone could wheedle a steak dinner in front of the TV out of her mom, it was her dad. "Good luck. I'll see you later."

Jim kissed her cheek. "No hurry. Hey, I'm proud of you, dear. I think you'll make a great Historical Director, even if it's just for a while."

The praise meant a lot. "Thanks, Dad."

After letting Stratton put the office back into order, they left the office. "Where to?" he asked as they walked toward his car.

"I know we have some things to talk about, but I was hoping you wouldn't mind if we stopped by the Jackson house first. The realtor said that she'd be available this evening if we wanted to look at it."

"That sounds great. Why don't you give her a call, then maybe we could find a steak dinner of our own tonight? It sounds like we have quite a few things to celebrate."

Joanne laughed. "Men and their steaks! You bet! After today's crazy events, I'm ready for anything."

Chapter Twelve

"This place is huge, Jo," Stratton said as they began to tour the grounds of the historic home.

Joanne nodded, and then turned her attention back to Mrs. Jamison, the realtor. Mrs. Jamison had been able to meet them at the Jackson home as soon as Joanne had called her.

"It is rather large," Mrs. Jamison said to Stratton. "It seemed especially that way when it was built in 1863. A Mr. Christopher Jackson, a wealthy textile owner, built it for his large family of seven children. Through the years, one or another descendent has lived here. From what I understand, most of the Jackson family finally left the area in the late seventies."

"And now?"

Mrs. Jamison waved a hand toward an overgrown

thicket of bushes. "Now, well, you see what it looks like. I think an aunt who lived in Florida let it become a duplex of sorts in the eighties, but that didn't work out."

They walked to the front porch and stood at the front door, which was propped open to let in some fresh air. Stratton glanced at the worn paint and the sagging floorboards. "I guess not."

"Now that it's on the market, quite a few people have plans for this place," Mrs. Jamison said sadly. "I don't know how much longer it will be standing."

"So I've heard," Joanne muttered. She placed a hand on the porch railing and tried to look at the house objectively, not through the eyes of a historian. The state of the house really did speak for itself. "Stratton, I know it's run down, but I really think this house could be beautiful one day."

Stratton smiled at her words but said nothing.

They entered the house, and after briefly outlining the floor plan, Mrs. Jamison took a seat by the door and told them to take their time looking around.

A marble entry with a dusty chandelier graced the foyer. Dark woodwork and crown molding lent a somewhat elegant touch. Heavy faded maroon curtains prevented light from entering. "Isn't it lovely?" Joanne asked as she pulled back one of the curtains to get a better look at the window frame. "Imagine what it looked like at the turn of the century."

Stratton looked skeptical. "Honestly, I'm having a

hard time envisioning this room as anything other than worn down."

"Come on, look at this alcove, at the woodwork!"

"I see it, all right."

Joanne detected a hint of sarcasm in his words, but chose to ignore them. She became more and more entranced as they toured the home. Each of the two floors was divided into one small room after another, each one cozier than the last. Stratton trailed behind her, and dutifully inspected each thing that she pointed out.

"If you bought this place, Joanne, you'd have to do something about the floor plan. I feel like I'm in a rat's maze."

"Ha, ha."

He coughed. "And these window treatments have got to go. I think a family of moths has been dining on them for some time."

It was getting easier and easier to ignore his barbs. She couldn't resist the aura of history and belonging that she felt in each room. When they walked into what had once been the master bedroom, the fireplace immediately captivated her. "Oh, look at this!" she gasped. "Wouldn't that be wonderful, to enjoy a fire while sitting in bed?"

Stratton looked bemused. "Joanne, is this your first time here?"

"This is the first time inside, but I've looked in the windows and walked around the outside quite a few times." She shrugged. "I don't know why exactly, but I really love this old place."

He smiled at her words. "I think there's a reason you studied art history and architecture in college. You can truly appreciate this house."

"I guess so. I'm so excited about this opportunity. I think the Historical Society will be a good place for me. I'm glad I accepted that job."

They continued to wander. It looked as though the original Mr. Jackson had accommodated each child in the house; there were at least eight bedrooms. While small by today's standards, some no bigger than a large walk-in closet, it was amazing to be in a house that was built for such a large amount of people.

However, Stratton did point out the obvious difference between today's architecture and the turn of the century's: bathrooms. There were only two for the entire family to share. "Imagine the fights over this place in the morning," he teased.

Joanne shook her head. "I don't know if I can. We grew up with four baths for seven people, and I thought that was hard!"

Finally, they walked back outside. Joanne resolutely strode towards the storm cellar door that was directly behind the kitchen door. The large wooden doors were made of planks that were faded and warped. A large black chain and open padlock lay to the left. "This is the way to the basement, Stratton," she said. "And from what I've learned, it's also the place where the slaves were hidden during the war."

There was no other choice but to pry open the door and walk down. Stratton trotted back to his car, retrieved a flashlight from his trunk, and then helped Joanne pull open the doors that had long since been rusted shut.

As they pulled the doors back, a cool burst of air and a tunnel of darkness met them. Although it looked foreboding, Joanne felt as if the cavern was beckoning her closer. She looked at the line of old stone steps with some misgiving. The top stones looked damp in the light, and were obviously built haphazardly, and only seemed to be pressed into the earth. They led downward in a steep path. Who knew what condition they were in now, two hundred years later?

Stratton shined the flashlight into the cellar. "Do you still want to give it a try?"

There really was only one answer. "Of course."

Joanne stepped down, gingerly touching each step before placing her full weight on it. Stratton stayed by her side, securely holding her elbow with one hand and the flashlight with the other.

The air smelled musty, like the earth. A chill swept through Joanne when they reached the bottom step. They stood in a small room; the walls only rose about six feet, and were lined with rough-looking gray and slate colored stones. It was obvious they were only held together by sheer will; no mortar was evident anywhere. The room led towards two small, narrow portals, and finally in the back of one room lay a cramped alcove, only about four feet high. Joanne braced her hands on her knees as she crept further. The dirt floor was cold and clammy under her feet.

Eventually it would be possible to add electricity and lights to the cramped maze of rooms. However, for now, the small enclosure made her feel caged in and claustrophobic.

Joanne glanced at Stratton. He, too, seemed interested in the design of the cellar. He shined the flashlight along the back wall. A line of bricks, obviously newer than the stones that lined the wall, made Joanne's heart jump. There was the passage that Tilly and others had made mention of. Finally Joanne found herself looking at the reason she was here—the very hiding place of slaves in this Underground Station.

Without thinking, Joanne crept forward and placed her hands along the lining of the bricks. "This was it, Stratton," she gasped. "This was where the Jacksons had guided the slaves to hide."

The bricked-up section was small, only about two feet by four. It was easy to imagine a person creeping through the opening and hiding on the other side. There were rumors that the Jacksons had held some people in this area for a day or two at a time. How frightened those people must have been, crouching in the dark and waiting for the next conductor to lead them to another safehouse. Joanne glanced above her.

"Shine the flashlight on the ceiling, would you? I wonder if there are still marks from torches or lanterns?"

Stratton did as she asked, but only shadows illuminated.

"I wonder if we hired an archaeologist to come in and dig; perhaps he or she would be able to . . ." Her voice trailed off. Suddenly, she voiced what was in her heart. "I think I want to actually own this house, Stratton. I've got to make sure that it's not torn down and forgotten."

Stratton reached out and pulled her closer. "I know you do. We'll make sure nothing happens to it. I promise."

Joanne rested her head against his chest and felt the reassuring, steady heartbeat. She brought her hands up to circle his waist, and felt one of his arms do the same. Stratton was warm, and solid, and comforting. And more importantly, he was honest. She could believe his promise; she could count on his optimism. But more than that, she could believe him. And that made her believe in herself.

"Thank you," she said simply, although there was so much more she wanted to say. However, the words caught in her throat; her emotion was too high.

On their way out, the couple stopped to talk to Mrs. Jamison, the realtor, who was doing a crossword puzzle near the front door.

"Thanks again," Joanne said sincerely. "I'm so glad

that you were able to let us visit. This house is a treasure; it has so much history and promise."

"You're very welcome, my dear," the old lady said with a sad smile. "I just wish others felt the same."

Stratton gestured toward the sign in front of the house. "Is that a done deal?"

Mrs. Jamison shook her head. "It is true that Payton Chase is interested in the land, and that he does want to build a convenience store here." Then she leaned forward. "But I'll tell you a secret. Mayor Kincaid and a few of the members of the town council aren't too crazy about it. They like the idea of keeping this area residential." She eyed Joanne shrewdly. "I have a feeling that they just need someone to spearhead an effort to save this place."

"Someone does need to do that! I can't believe that others would think that this place would be the best spot for a mini-mart," Joanne said.

"But no one has stepped forward to take charge, dear," Mrs. Jamison pointed out. "And Payton Chase might not run into any roadblocks if no one comes forward soon with a viable plan to save the house." She stood up and ran her fingers down her skirt to straighten it. "This home is not on a historic register. It just happens to be old and big."

"And full of history! Mrs. Jamison, you ought to go to the mayor and say something. How can you just sit by? Letting this place go and get torn down would be a travesty!"

The elder lady pursed her lips. "I'm just a realtor, trying to make ends meet, Joanne. What you're suggesting is going to take more effort than I am willing to give. I plan to retire in two years."

"But Mrs. Jamison—"

The elder lady gave Joanne a reproving look. "It's not my fault that the Jackson house is worn down and neglected, Joanne. I don't appreciate your insinuations."

"I'm sorry." Joanne immediately looked chagrined. "I didn't mean what I said that way. I guess I just can't help but be sad that this old building won't be around forever."

"Nothing stays the same, my dear," Mrs. Jamison said gently. "I thought after the fire you would have realized that."

"I should have, I'm sure of that," Joanne said. Stratton must have seen her slumped shoulders and bright eyes and knew she was about to cry, because he took her hand and squeezed it gently.

Mrs. Jamison noticed the gesture and raised her eyebrows. "Young man, I heard you're doing a good job in town. I'm glad you're here. Doc is a good man, but everyone needs to take a break sometimes. I'll be in to see you before long."

"I'll look forward to it," Stratton replied, then escorted Joanne out to the street after they said their good-byes.

As they approached his car, Joanne couldn't help

but turn around and look at the building again. "It's just such a shame, Stratton. Look at the dormers, and the lines on the front." She pointed to a sitting area on the east side of the structure. "The original owners used to have a trellis, and a rose garden here. Wouldn't it be a wonderful place to have tea on Sunday afternoons?"

Stratton tilted his head at the structure, and then glanced back at Joanne. "I don't believe I've ever had tea in my life, let alone in a rose garden," Stratton replied sardonically, "but I get your gist."

"It's going to be such a travesty to lose this place," she said again.

Stratton held the door open for her, then glanced up at the house as he got into the driver's side. "Why don't you actually try and buy it, then?" he asked quietly.

"Really?"

"Sure. Didn't you get some money from the insurance company?"

The same conversation that she had shared with her father buzzed in her head. "Well, I did get some money, but not enough for this."

"You could get a loan from the bank," he said practically.

"What would I do with such a large place anyway? You heard Mrs. Jamison—no one's interested in looking at it but me."

"How about making the back of the first floor a little

museum? You could live in most of the house, but have part of it open so everyone can learn about the history of the home." His voice warmed as he continued. "You could give tours there a few days a month, or only to people who call for appointments. I bet with your new job, you'd be able to incorporate the two."

Her voice became dreamy. "It would be perfect, wouldn't it? I could renovate two or three of those bedrooms into a living area. Hey, I could even serve you tea one day on the terrace." Her voice warmed to the idea. "Maybe even part of it could be a community room—I know my mom is always looking for somewhere interesting to have her meetings."

Stratton smiled. "That house has promise, huh? I think you should look into it."

Joanne considered his words. "Maybe, I don't know. Everything is suddenly happening so fast." She stopped then, and thought of the words she had spoken the night before. She glanced at Stratton and remembered the feel of his broad shoulders and strong arms, and swallowed hard. "Hey, speaking of promises . . ."

"Yes?" he said, as he turned the key in the ignition.

"Stratton, I meant what I said last night about the two of us. I do think there's something between us that's worth nurturing."

He turned to face her. She recalled the feel of his cheek against hers, how she had traced the line of his jaw with her finger the other night.

"And?"

Boy, he wasn't making this any easier for her. She looked down at the hands she had clasped in her lap and then said softly, "Um, I've always been a little unsure of myself and a little frightened of relationships. And, uh, Payton didn't help much."

She paused, and not hearing a reply, finally raised her head to glance at him. Stratton's expression was tender and patient, as if he had all the time in the world to listen to her try to explain herself. She cleared her throat. "Um, I guess I'm trying to tell you, Stratton, that I might need to go a little slow with this relationship thing. I like you a lot, I really do, it's just that . . ."

He reached out a hand to her. "You just want to go slow?"

She could feel the heat rising to her cheeks again as she nodded. Oh, what would he think of her? Of her words? Did she sound immature and gauche? Did he find her ridiculous? Joanne forced herself to meet his eyes. They had a sparkle in them that caught her off guard.

"How slow do you want to go?" His voice was low, mesmerizing.

Confused, she asked, "What do you mean?"

"I mean, may I kiss you? Am I allowed to tell you that I think you're wonderful, can I call you often . . ." He flashed a smile. "When we're in this slow mode?"

Was he teasing her? "Stratton, I'm just saying . . ."

His hand brushed a stray hair from her cheek, and

then followed the path of her hair down her back. Her spine tingled at his contact. "I understand, Jo. It's okay. We can do anything you want."

"Oh." Her heart jumped. Gosh, he *did* understand. She forced herself to reply. "I think all of those things you wanted to do would be just fine," she squeaked.

"All right, then." he murmured, "Just so long as we understand each other . . ." Stratton leaned forward, his mouth inches from hers.

She could feel the heat from his breath. Her own caught. "Understanding is very important."

"Good. That is very good," he whispered against her lips, then finally closed the gap to kiss her.

Joanne raised her own hands to hold him close. It felt so good to be close to somebody, somebody that she trusted. She kissed him back with passion.

Minutes later they moved apart.

"You okay?" Stratton asked, his hands grazing her shoulders.

"Oh, yes," Joanne said, then smiled at her words. Being near him was so easy, so right.

Then, realizing they were still parked on the street, she attempted to direct their thoughts to other things. "Are you hungry? Do you still want to get a bite to eat?"

"Absolutely," Stratton said with a grin as he sat back and then pulled the car away from the curb. "I believe that we have a lot to celebrate."

"Let's go to the Old Mill Grill then. It's on the bike

path. Afterward, we can walk on the path, if you want."

"I want to, Jo," he said as he clasped her hand.

"Look at the fireflies," Stratton said later that evening as they strolled down the path. The day had slowly faded into early evening, and both seemed content to watch the stars appear one by one and enjoy the quiet of the trail. The fierce chirping of the crickets rang in the air, punctuated every so often by the croak of a frog or the shrill call of a jay.

Joanne couldn't remember ever having such a wonderful evening. It seemed magical to be with Stratton, especially now that it seemed that they had resolved some of their issues. For the first time in days she felt calm and secure, and was eager to savor every bit of it. She gasped in pleasure as the first fireflies of the night appeared, twinkling like their own personal stars. "My friend Julie is from Texas. Did you know that they don't have fireflies there?"

"To be honest, I never thought about it."

"Can you imagine? Just seeing them put me in a good mood. They give me hope—if the fireflies can keep coming back to Ohio every year, even after a hard winter, then I can keep trying, too."

When she stopped and pointed to several others glinting in a thicket of trees nearby, Stratton didn't seem to mind. "I used to catch them and put them in jars. Did you ever do that?"

"Cameron did, but I didn't." Joanne said with a touch of embarrassment. "It sounds funny, but I just wanted them to be free."

He chuckled. "Never? It was so cool to watch them up close . . ."

Memories of the flies in jars, and of her brothers and Denise teasing her about being the firefly advocate came back suddenly. "I just hated the thought of them dying, that's all."

"Well, they're thriving here," Stratton observed, pointing to another group of insects several feet in front of them.

She laughed. "You're right. These are just like our own private set of Christmas lights."

Stratton moved closer and curled his arm around her shoulders. "Just for us."

He was right. No one else was around. Again she was drawn to Stratton, felt his pull. "We could celebrate, right here, under our lights . . ." he murmured.

"Celebrate? But—"

He pressed his fingers to her lips. "Shh. I don't want to hear about it."

"But—"

"I just want to be with you, Joanne. That's reason enough." He reached out and fingered her long hair. The contact between them made her feel wanted, assured. And that feeling gave her the same sense of wonder as the fireflies.

When his fingers trailed the bare skin of her arm,

she shivered. And when his hands reached for hers, she readily intertwined her fingers with his. Just that contact created an awareness in Joanne for more between them.

Stratton bent down and nuzzled her neck. "Do you think you should make a wish?"

"A wish?" It was hard to think when his lips pressed against the nape of her neck.

"Why not?" he murmured. "Isn't there something you want?"

Joanne closed her eyes. *I wish I could look forward to this every day*, she thought to herself. *I wish I could look forward to feeling this secure and wanted every day.* She opened her eyes and met Stratton's gaze. "Did you make a wish, too?"

His lips curved at her question. "No."

"Why not?"

"My wish has already come true."

Joanne raised her arms to encircle his neck. His drew around her waist and tugged her closer. Then finally his lips met hers and there was nothing to say.

Chapter Thirteen

Ten days later, Joanne found herself getting ready to defend the fate of Jackson House against her old boyfriend. She shook her head. Who would have thought a month ago that she would be in this situation?

She glanced around the auditorium. The town hall was crowded. It seemed as if every person in Payton who had nothing better to do had decided to claim a seat and watch the ensuing verbal contest between herself and Payton Chase.

Feeling uncomfortable, she shifted the skirt of her suit. How had she gotten herself so far into this mess, anyway? Why hadn't she kept her big mouth shut? One moment she was just Joanne Reece, fired temporary worker . . .

Now all of the sudden she felt like some bizarre Florence Nightingale, sent to save an abandoned building from destruction.

And she didn't know what to do. All she did know was that she didn't want to just sit back and let the Jackson house get torn down without a fight. Not that she had expected to be the chosen freedom fighter. She bit her lip and reconsidered. Okay, maybe she had volunteered, but she didn't have to be happy about it.

However, no matter how it happened, here she was, with a little nametag stuck to her chest that proclaimed her the new interim director of the Payton Historical and Preservation Society.

The new title felt strange and scary. Joanne had a feeling that her mother would know more about how to run the society than she would. Actually, a lot of people would probably do better. But her mother wasn't sitting on the stage with her. She was in the middle of the audience with her brothers, Denise, and her dad.

Joanne squinted into the audience. If she wasn't mistaken, Mary Beth's parents were there too, and both families seemed to be chatting comfortably, almost as if they were at the movies, waiting for the show to begin.

Joanne continued to look around the auditorium. There, front and center, sat Stratton, looking handsome and debonair as usual. And he seemed to be holding court with a group of elderly women. Visions of Bingo night came flooding back. Only Stratton would have been able to win a Bingo game and a dozen hearts in one night.

She was just about to look away when Stratton glanced up and caught her eye. The corners of his mouth tilted upward and his right hand made a "thumbs-up" sign. Joanne's body relaxed immediately. No matter what, Stratton Sawyer supported her, and that meant the world.

She was just about to scan the audience again when the mayor entered the room, followed by Payton, looking smug and ridiculous in a crested blazer. The two men sat down next to her behind the podium.

"Hello, Mayor, Payton," Joanne said.

"Joanne," Mayor Kincaid said warmly.

"Miss Reece."

Joanne blinked in surprise at Payton's cold demeanor. Had things really changed so much between them? Irritation pricked at her thoughts. "I won't ask how you are doing, Payton," she said, peeved. "I can tell you are still the same as ever."

"Listen, Joanne, just because you're now homeless—"

"Homeless! I'll have you know—"

"Children," Mayor Kincaid interrupted. "Perhaps we'd all do better to pay attention to the reason for our meeting."

"But, Mayor—" Joanne protested and then stopped as she realized that the crowd of hundreds had become silent and were avidly listening to their conversation. "Of course. I'm sorry."

That seemed to be enough for the mayor. He stood up and approached the podium slowly, and then adjusted the microphone to his five-foot-six-inch height. The microphone made a screeching sound as he tapped it a few times for good measure. "Hello, everybody. Glad you're here," he said in his usual understated way. "I guess there's not a lot on TV tonight, huh?"

A couple of chuckles met his barb. "As you know, the reason for this little meeting was to give everyone a chance to be heard before the town council and vote about the proposed zoning change on the land on Mill Avenue." He cleared his throat. "Y'all know, the old Jackson house."

Joanne glanced at the audience. Most were listening to the mayor intently; and several were nodding as he spoke. It looked as if people were not only curious about the meeting; they also were interested in the outcome. A flutter of nervousness rushed through her as she tried to concentrate on the mayor's words.

"Two people are going to speak today, both of whom have some personal interest in the outcome of these proceedings. I invite all of you to listen closely and to wait to ask your questions at the end of our meeting." He paused for a moment, rocking back and forth on the pads of his feet while he waited for his words to sink in. "Okay? Well, then, Payton Chase will begin."

Payton stood up and strode the six feet to the podium with purpose. Joanne forced herself to look composed as he flashed one of his trademark hundred-watt smiles.

Then she jumped as he pounded his fist on the podium. "Don't y'all want Payton to be a better place for our children? Don't we want our grandchildren to grow up and be proud to live in Ohio?"

Joanne thought that sounded a little confusing, given the fact that Payton himself had no children to speak of. Then she focused her attention back on the speaker.

". . . It's time to improve our town, make it more convenient for everyone to get a quart of milk, or a carton of wholesome eggs, or candy after school," Payton whispered. "We have that chance. We have the chance to let everyone in the downtown area to have access to basic necessities of life! Let's take this chance, together!"

Every time Payton had emphasized the word 'chance' Joanne had winced. She seemed to recall them having a 'chance' together. But calling candy a basic necessity seemed far-fetched. Wasn't that laying it on a little thick?

Joanne sighed and watched the audience as Payton droned on. A certain satisfaction rose in her as she saw that others were also trying to figure out the correlation between mini-marts and freedom in the Constitution.

Joanne glanced at Stratton. He was looking straight at her. When their gazes met, he winked. She returned the wink with a small smile of her own, then glanced at the large clock that hung in the back of the room. By her calculations, Payton should have finished a few minutes ago. Joanne glanced at the mayor.

Mayor Kincaid looked annoyed. Everyone in the town knew that the mayor was a stickler for punctuality and his place of importance in a meeting. Payton was making a tactical error by ignoring both. Joanne forced herself to listen to what surely had to be the end of Payton's speech.

"And now, my fellow Americans, I ask you to consider the new jobs that will come to our town because of this development! And remember also, that this mini-mart could be the cornerstone of progress for Payton!"

Grumblings were heard in the audience. Then, Mrs. McCluskey stood up. "You mean we could soon have mini-marts all over this town?" she called out.

"Now, Mrs. Mac, you know that is not what I'm talking about," Payton said sharply.

"I've been getting my eggs just fine for twenty-three years at the grocery," she continued.

Groans followed her outburst. "I don't want to go to some newfangled mini-what-ever you call it."

"Yeah!" others called out.

Mayor Kincaid stood up. "Your time's up, son," he

said to Payton as he pointed to the clock. "Was up six and a half minutes ago."

"All right, Mayor, just a second," Payton said, then turned to the crowd again. "We can do this! We can promote progress! Together, we can improve Payton!"

The mayor harrumphed as he stepped in front of Payton Chase. "It is now time to let Joanne Reece speak," he said as he pointed to the clock. Then his voice softened. "Jo, you ready?"

"Yes, Mr. Mayor."

Joanne stood up and gingerly walked to the podium. She looked out into the audience and saw her parents' calm, encouraging smiles, just like they had given her when she'd had to give that valedictorian speech when she graduated high school so many years ago.

"Hi everybody," she said quietly into the microphone.

"I can't hear you! Speak up, girl," Mrs. Mac called out.

Giggles erupted in the audience. "Yes, ma'am," she said and then gathered up her courage and began to speak. "I agree with Payton. I think we could use some new buildings and stores in our town. In fact, it would be nice to have another convenience store in the north side of town. But I don't think these stores should be at the expense of the buildings that are already standing."

Joanne looked earnestly at the crowd. "Now, I know

that Jackson house is run-down. I agree that some see it as an eyesore. But lots of people, lots of you in the audience, as a matter of fact, think it was an Underground Railroad Station. The tax records and the history of the site are showing that to be true too. Don't you think that's enough to try to save it?"

As several people murmured agreement, Joanne took a deep breath and relaxed her hands that had been gripping the sides of the podium tightly. "There's not many towns that can boast to have such a place, and I for one, think we should be pretty proud of it."

She continued to explain her reasonings and then conscientiously stopped a full thirty seconds early. The mayor looked pleased.

Mayor Kincaid stepped forward. "Now everyone, as promised, I'll let you ask some questions."

Several began to talk. Payton was asked to explain in detail his schedule for the mini-mart. Then, Joanne was called on to add details about her findings about the house. Finally, Doc Whitman stood up. "Joanne, exactly how do you propose to save this building?"

She shifted uncomfortably. "Well, most of you know that my shop and apartment burned down a month ago."

"Yes."

"I haven't spoken to many people about this yet, but everybody I would need to talk to is in this room. Here goes: I thought I would use my insurance money to purchase the Jackson home and begin refurbishing it."

"So, your plan is actually self-serving," Payton spat out.

Enough was enough. She had had enough of Payton's snide accusations. She turned to him and spoke in her firmest tone. "Payton, you need to let me speak."

Payton responded by letting out an exaggerated sigh. "Honestly, Joanne, I don't think there's anyone here that needs to hear another crazy plan of yours . . ."

Oh, that was a tone that she had heard way too often. Joanne opened her mouth to retort, but was cut off by Doctor Whitman.

"Let the girl speak, Payton," Doc said sternly.

"Honestly Payton, where are your manners?" Mrs. Barbara Kelly stood up and waved a hand at him. "No wonder Joanne decided she had had enough of you!"

Payton's cheeks flushed. "Now wait a minute, I dumped her . . ."

That seemed to be all that Jim Reece had needed to hear. He stood up. "Now listen here, you no-good, no-account—"

"Dad!" Joanne gasped, horrified.

Pandemonium broke out. Jim marched up to the podium. Stratton and her brothers looked eager to follow. Mrs. Mac seemed to have a bone to pick with everyone, and looked as if she was telling them so. Even

Tilly, the lady from Bingo night, had gotten into the action. Payton was defending himself to several people at the same time. Joanne tried to reason with her dad, then finally sat down, appalled at what had happened.

Mayor Kincaid was not happy. He marched up to the podium, pulled open the single drawer that was located just under the table top, grabbed his gavel, and pounded it three times. "Be quiet, everyone!"

The crowd stood stunned at his outburst.

"Now, I for one, am interested in what Joanne has to say. The rest of you, sit down and be quiet."

One hundred people immediately did as they were told.

"Now, Joanne, tell us once again about your plans, without interruptions."

Joanne stood up again. After giving Payton a cold look, she began to speak as clearly as she was able. "As I was saying, I thought I could buy the house, refurbish part of it to live in, and then begin to make the back part of it a small museum for visitors and schoolchildren, say, once a month." Joanne bit her lip nervously, and kept her eyes on the understanding ones of the mayor. "That way, the house would not be the eyesore it is right now; I would have a place to live; and the Jackson house would retain its integrity. People would still be able to see where the slaves had been hidden, and the hard work that the Jacksons did in order to promote freedom for all people, but it wouldn't really cost anyone a lot of money."

Mayor Kincaid spoke. "You would do all of this on your own?"

Joanne swallowed. "Well, I thought I'd write a grant to some historical societies to help pay for the museum part, and maybe even charge people a dollar to see the place, that could be used for upkeep, or maybe even some further research on Underground Stations in Payton. Of course, that would be up to the Historical Society."

Mayor Kincaid looked at Joanne with respect. "Thank you, Joanne," he said loudly, then added quietly, "Well done, my dear," as she stepped back toward her seat.

Finally the mayor thanked everybody for coming and told them that an answer would be decided in two days' time. Seeing that nobody looked especially eager to leave, he drummed his fingers on the podium and then pointed to the overhead clock.

"Well, everybody, it's nine P.M. and time to go see what's happening on TV. Good night."

As Joanne stepped off of the stage, she had no idea what was going to happen. All she did know was that she had presented herself in a good way to the town, for once. She hadn't bungled words or tripped or fallen. She had been able to relay her plans in a clear, concise manner. And she had even stood up to Payton Chase, with an audience looking on.

Joanne grinned at Stratton as he stepped forward, arms ready to engulf her in a hug.

"You did pretty good, Jo," he said, pride evident in his eyes.

"I was so nervous."

"I know you were, but you didn't look that way," he said as he took her hands. "I promise, no one could have done a better job up there tonight."

The compliments made her feel giddy. "Thanks," she said merrily, then squealed as he picked her up and swung her in a circle. She held on tight and laughed in exhilaration.

"Joanne," her mother called. "Let's go home and celebrate your triumph!"

Still locked in Stratton's embrace, she answered. "But Stratton—"

"Needs to come over, too," Jim interrupted. "You're a couple, aren't you?"

Stratton grinned. "We're coming. We'll be right behind you." Slowly he lowered Joanne to rest against him. "I think things are going fairly well," he said, a smile playing along the corners of his lips.

"I agree," she whispered, reaching up to kiss his cheek. She felt so good nestled against him; she didn't want to leave the security of his embrace.

"We better get out of here. Your family's waiting and Mayor Kincaid looks as if he's ready to turn off the lights."

"All right. But promise me that we can celebrate later, by ourselves?"

Stratton's gaze darkened. "Anytime you want, I'll be available."

"I'll remember that, Stratton," Joanne said as he took her hand and then led the way out the door.

Chapter Fourteen

Things began to happen quickly after the evening of the council meeting. Two days later, the council voted unanimously to refuse Payton Chase's request for the change in zoning. Hours after that decision, Mayor Kincaid himself called Joanne at her parents' and said it should be her civic duty to begin the process of buying, refurbishing, and organizing Payton's Underground Railroad Museum.

Joanne agreed without hesitation. Then she sat down with her father, and began to navigate the legal pathways required to own her new home. In the days that followed, architects were interviewed and hired, and Mrs. Jamison, the realtor, stopped by to give her the keys.

Jeremy and Kevin removed the FOR SALE sign from the front of the house with pleasure.

Through it all, Stratton was supportive, but distant, to Joanne's point of view. Granted, now that the town had supported him wholeheartedly, he was busier than ever. But Joanne couldn't help but feel that there was something missing between them. She felt the loss, but persuaded herself to believe that perhaps she had never clearly conveyed her feelings towards him.

In addition, she gradually became used to her new position at the historical society. She found a true friend in Missy, who just happened to know more about the actual day-to-day business of managing a museum than she had originally let on. Joanne knew that they were going to do great things together.

Before she knew it, everything was final, and she had a new house. She moved into the one room that was liveable and got ready for the real flurry of activity that was inevitable; her family had decided to become wholeheartedly involved in refurbishing the house.

With fresh visions of life with her brother Cameron and Mary Beth and their hunt for treasure in her mind, she stepped aside and let them have their way. She knew from experience that it was easier to give in gracefully from the beginning.

Unfortunately, Stratton didn't have those memories to draw from. He seemed to be caught off-guard by the way her parents and siblings made themselves at home. Maybe that had something to do with his distance, too, she mused. She vowed to try to spend some time alone with him during the next few days.

A month later, Stratton sat on the bottom step of the stairs and regarded everyone with dismay. It seemed as though he'd been spending more time at Joanne's than at his own apartment. Unfortunately, it was never just the two of them. He recalled their date to the country club and their walk together by the river afterward with fondness. He would give a lot to do that again. Time just seemed to be moving so quickly for them both.

He winced as he heard someone drop a hammer, followed by a stream of conversation in the next room. That was their problem: he and Joanne needed to be alone.

There were always too many people in the house, regardless of how big it was, Stratton thought to himself as he observed the organized chaos around him. Joanne's father was working on the computer system, her mother, the finishing touches in the living room.

Joanne's brothers Jeremy, Kevin, and Cameron were arguing over the best way to install the new kitchen sink, and her sister-in-law Mary Beth and a friend of hers were upstairs dusting the bedrooms.

It seemed as if he was the only one not working frantically on a job. And although he wouldn't tell anyone, he liked it that way. He had been up late the night before, Mrs. Asner's baby having decided to arrive two weeks early, at three in the morning. Although the delivery had gone like clockwork, he was still reeling from the adrenaline he always felt when a new life entered the world.

Besides, a part of him felt like his job was to watch over Joanne, to keep her from hurting herself. By the circles under her eyes and the wooden way she was functioning, he would hazard a guess that she hadn't had much more sleep than himself last night. The museum was to open to the first guests, the mayor and city council members, around two o'clock the next day. He hoped that he would be able to get her to sleep for at least eight hours between now and then.

Suddenly the idea of getting a hold of her for a moment sounded awfully good. When she passed in front of him again, he reached out an arm from his spot at the foot of the stairs and caught hold of her.

"Stratton," she gasped.

"Shh," he said, gently pulling her down next to him.

"I've got so many things to do."

"I know," he murmured as he wrapped his other arm around her, her slim body feeling so good against his.

"I mean it. I've got to go make cookies, and address my next set of mailers, and take a minute and organize my room."

"Jo—"

A look of panic entered her eyes. "And then, there's the—"

"Joanne."

At his voice, she turned to him. "I guess I've gone a little crazy, hmm? It's times like these when sitting on Mom's chair watching *Pillow Talk* with my foot propped up doesn't sound so bad."

"Speaking of which, I heard from your sister-in-law that you haven't even bought a bed yet. Where have you been sleeping?"

Joanne shrugged. "On an air mattress of Jeremy's in my bedroom with a blanket."

Concern etched his eyes. "Jo, I thought you were going to take a minute and buy a bed, at least."

"I haven't had a minute to do that. I've been concentrating on the museum. Mayor Kincaid calls all the time." She tiredly brushed a hand over the braid in her hair. "Stratton, the bed doesn't matter. It's not like I've had a moment to lay down, anyway."

That what was worried him. He leaned down, kissed her neck, and was pleased when she didn't pull away. "Tonight I'm going to change your schedule. We'll have an early dinner, then get you into bed by nine."

"Stratton, I've got the mayor coming tomorrow, and who knows what will happen the day after that!"

"And the day after that, too." He ran his fingers up and down her arms. "I've been on phone duty too, remember? I know the kind of press and phone calls you've been receiving—it sounds as if everyone is interested in this house now." He pressed a kiss to her forehead. "You've got to get some rest before everyone comes, or you're going to fall apart."

"Maybe you're right." At his look, she amended her words. "Okay, Doctor, I know you're right." A worried look entered her eyes. "By the way, have I remembered to thank you?"

"I think so, but you could thank me again." He moved his hands from her arms to her hair, and then nuzzled her neck. At first she tensed, but then he knew he had finally gotten to her when he felt her body relax against him. She felt supple and soft and smelled like Ivory soap. He was itching to be alone with her. "How about later tonight, after everyone else has gone?"

She pretended to consider. "I think I could probably try to fit you into my schedule."

He was prevented from replying by the appearance of Mary Beth on the upstairs landing. "Joanne, we're finished. Do you want to come up and take a look?"

Joanne craned her neck to look at Mary Beth. She wore a smile that said she knew exactly what had been going on between Joanne and Stratton. "Sure. I'll be right there."

Stratton let his hands linger as Joanne stood up. "I'm going to go work on your room, is that all right with you? If you're not going to get yourself organized, then I might as well try."

Distractedly, she looked at him. "All right, but I don't see why that matters."

Stratton shook his head as he watched her make her way back up the stairs and then greet her sister-in-law with a sunny smile. Joanne needed twenty-four-hour surveillance before she passed out. With a sigh, he stood up and made his way to the back of the house.

Along the way, he passed Mr. and Mrs. Reece, who had switched jobs and were currently sweeping the kitchen's wood floor and organizing the pantry. "Hi Stratton," Daphne said. "Would you like to give us a hand? We're trying to decide if Joanne's pantry should be completely alphabetized or not."

Envisioning Joanne trying to find the sugar in between the rice and cans of tomatoes was a scary thought. "I would leave the alphabetizing for another day," he said dryly. "I'm off to go make your daughter's bed and unpack her bags."

Jim looked pleased. "Good thinking."

Stratton grinned. A lot of other parents would be put off by the thought of a man sorting through their daughter's personal items. Not them.

As he opened her bedroom door, he winced at the sight that awaited him. It looked as if her bedroom was also now a storage area. Boxes of books, clothes, and shoes were stacked in the middle of the room, along with bags full of makeup, toiletries, and what looked to be a huge container of coffee. Leave it to Joanne to make sure she had her priorities in order.

He glanced towards the back of the room, in front of a tiny closet. There, three suitcases were open, and clothes were scattered all over the general vicinity. Boxes of antique figurines, Joanne's vanity case, and a bookcase of paperbacks lined the right side of the room. In the middle of it all lay a twin-sized air mattress with only two pillows, a single sheet, and a blanket strewn in the middle of it. Stratton's expression softened; he could imagine her sprawled in the middle of it last night.

He scanned the area for sheets, then finally found some pink ones peeking out of a suitcase. He grabbed them, tossed them on the bed, and then resolutely decided to get to work.

After Stratton remade the mattress, this time with two clean sheets, he began the long process of unpacking Joanne's suitcase and stuffing the clothes into various dresser drawers. Then he looked around the room. Things were starting to look better already.

Next it was time to figure out what to do with all of the old boxes and suitcases. There had to be an extra cabinet somewhere in the house. But when he opened the door, he was greeted by a frenzy of activity.

"Hey, Stratton," Cameron said, paintbrush in hand.

"Hey," he replied, carrying a suitcase out of the bedroom. "Any idea where there's room for all of this stuff?"

Cam shrugged. "You better take a look around. All I know is where I've been," he said with a grin.

"Thanks for nothing," Stratton joked, then made his

way towards the kitchen, and the adjoining butler's pantry. As he walked into the room, he spied Joanne perched on the top of an old rickety wooden ladder, polishing a chandelier in the formal dining area. Stratton felt as if his heart stopped for a moment. "What are you doing up there?"

Joanne glanced down at him. "Isn't it obvious?"

"Joanne, you have no business climbing up ladders, especially ones that look as old as this house. Why don't you get down and let me do that for you?"

"I think I can handle this, Stratton. What are you doing?"

"I've been trying to clear a path in your bedroom."

She grimaced. "How's it going?"

"Good enough. Get down now, why don't you?"

Mr. Reece appeared. "Stratton, don't worry about Joanne. I know she seems accident prone, but she's actually pretty nimble when it comes to heights."

"*Seems* accident prone?" Stratton repeated.

Even from her perch, Stratton could see Joanne rolling her eyes. "I'm fine. There's a coat closet off the kitchen. Maybe the suitcases could be temporarily stored in there."

"Fine."

"Don't worry about Joanne," Jim said as Stratton walked by. "You're here in case she does fall."

"But I'm getting tired of patching her up," he mumbled to himself. "I had other things in mind to do with her body besides heal it."

"Excuse me?" Daphne said as Stratton entered the kitchen.

There were really way too many Reeces in this house. "Nothing. I was just looking for a place to store a couple of suitcases."

Within minutes, Daphne and he had uncovered a large closet in the butler's pantry. He then began the task of carting the bags and boxes out of Joanne's room to the kitchen area. Each time he passed Joanne on the ladder he checked on her warily.

Then, of course, in his mind, the inevitable happened. Joanne stood on her tiptoes to wipe off a spot, the ladder swayed, and she fell. A sudden crash, then a moan was heard throughout the house. Stratton dropped the box he was carting to the garage and rushed over.

His breath caught as he saw her in a crumpled heap on the floor.

"Jo," he said as he came forward. "Jo, can you hear me?"

"Stratton," she moaned.

Within minutes, the foyer was crowded with seven other people, eager to lend a hand. "Call a doctor," Julie, one of Mary Beth's friends, said.

"He *is* the doctor!" another exclaimed.

He ignored them all, and knelt down next to her. Immediately, he began to gingerly examine her body for broken bones. "What hurts? Can you move?"

"I think I'm all right, except for my hands." Joanne

said weakly. "I grabbed hold of the ladder when I stumbled, and didn't let go."

Stratton reached out for her hands, and grimaced when he saw they were bleeding and filled with at least thirty splinters of wood.

"I'll take care of you, sweetheart, don't worry," he said automatically. Then, he looked at the group. "Could someone go out to my car? I've got a bag in there full of supplies. I think I can take care of Joanne's hands here."

Kevin volunteered immediately, while the others continued to look on as Stratton helped Joanne stand up. He carefully watched her as she tested her strength.

She winced as one of her hands accidentally pressed against the floor. "Ouch. This really hurts."

"I know, baby," he said, and then picked her up without thinking. "Let's go into the kitchen. I'll take care of you."

Her eyes met his. She seemed to have no problem letting him hold her in front of her family. "I'm sorry to be so much trouble."

Suddenly it was if they were the only two people in the room. "It's no trouble," he murmured as he leaned down to kiss her cheek. "I need to get used to it anyway."

She gave him a tremulous smile. "Why do you say that?"

"I'll tell you later." Then, realizing once again that

they were surrounded, he abruptly made an executive decision. "Do you mind if I do something?"

She shook her head. "Do anything you want."

Stratton groaned at her words. How he wished he was able to do that! Resolutely, he turned to her family and spoke, doing his best to keep a straight face. "I need y'all to leave."

Daphne stepped forward. "But—"

"Joanne's hurting and worn out. She needs some peace and quiet." He looked beseechingly at Cameron, hoping he would understand exactly what he meant. "Would you mind?"

A smile curved Cam's lips. "Not at all. Come on, Mom, Dad, let's get going."

"But," Daphne sputtered again.

"Did I tell you what Mary Beth and I have been doing to the house?" Cam asked his parents. "You know, it's so hard to describe, I think you'll just have to come on by."

"We'd love to have you," Mary Beth chimed in, a twinkle in her eyes.

"We'll go, too," Kevin said meaningfully, glancing at the others. "I can't wait to see the place."

Within minutes, Stratton settled Joanne on a kitchen chair and was breathing a sigh of relief at the blessed silence. He owed Joanne's siblings big time. "You doing okay?"

Joanne held her hands up like paws. "More or less," she said, watching him wash his hands. Then she tilted her head. "Hey, what were you going to say earlier, about needing to get used to me?"

"Well, someone's got to take care of you."

"Is that what you want to do? Take care of me?"

Hardly. "No, silly. I want to marry you."

Joanne's eyes widened. "You do?"

"I do," he said calmly, then reached for his bag that Kevin had left on the table.

"I do, too," she breathed.

He bent down and tenderly kissed her lips. "I love you, Joanne Reece. I think you're terrific."

"I love you too."

"Then, ah, will you let me take care of your hands?"

Startled, she looked at her palms. They looked jagged and pretty cut up. "All right," she said weakly.

Ready to get to work, Stratton retrieved antiseptic, tweezers, and some lotion to deaden her hands.

She closed her eyes when he began to get to work. "Um, would you care if we lived here?"

"I would live anywhere with you." He glanced around the kitchen, and thought of the gleaming woodwork in the entryway, the fresh roses, the shabby furniture . . . it held the promise of a bright future in every corner. And beyond that, a family that loved the woman he loved, and who had taken the time and energy to take him in and make him feel welcome.

The contrast with his childhood apartment and lifestyle was staggering. "I think I could probably handle living here," he said as he carefully pulled a splinter from her hand.

Joanne's expression warmed. "As long as you're sure . . ."

"I'm sure, honey."

"Then I can't wait to marry you."

"Good," Stratton said as he leaned down and lightly kissed the inside of her wrist. "I was hoping you'd say that."

Epilogue

"Well, you did it; you saved the Jackson house," Stratton said as they looked around the old house several days later.

"*I* didn't really, it just all worked out," Joanne said modestly, holding her bandaged hands close to her chest.

He guided her to the living room, where they sat down on the lone couch. "I guess you could say that," Stratton replied with a knowing grin. "I guess you could say that Payton just happened to back out of the deal, that the community just happened to realize that this old place had historical significance, and that the ladies at the museum just happened to need you as their interim director."

Joanne blushed as she heard Stratton's version of

all of the things she had accomplished in such a short time. "I think saying I had a whole lot to do with getting that job is not quite right. Those ladies just needed a new person in charge of the historical museum and society and I was available." She grinned at the memory. "And I'm pretty sure they were harboring a healthy dose of fear for kindergarteners at the time."

"Uh huh."

Joanne reddened at his skeptical look. "You're not believing all of this for a minute, are you?"

"No."

A smile slowly lit her expression. "It was worth a try. I'm really glad it all happened like this. I don't know what I would have done if I was still a temporary worker. I was a pretty pitiful one. It just wasn't for me."

He chuckled. "I think several people felt that way."

"Oh, you, just because I had a couple of bad experiences . . ."

"Means that it's good that you've finally found a better vocation."

Joanne smiled at him. "I guess you're right."

She glanced around the old house. Plans were already under way for a local archaeologist from the University of Cincinnati to dig in the cellar to try to uncover artifacts.

In addition, Joanne was due to work with a team of grant writers later that week to go over some proposals for the Historical Society.

But first off, she was going to use the rest of her insurance money to finish the remodeling of the first and second floors. Even though the area for tours was in pretty good shape, she was looking forward to living in a place that felt like a home.

And she was thrilled to have a home again, one with personality and substance.

Yes, things were looking up, pretty much, anyway. She slid a sideways look at Stratton. He noticed and wrapped an arm around her and held her close. Once again she was struck by how beautiful his hands were, how handsome he was. Memories flashed of her first sight of him, standing over her in that examining room. She was so glad she had met him, had fallen in love with him. As the silence between them stretched, she pursed her lips.

"Stratton, I'm sorry, I've been so involved in my plans, I haven't even asked you lately about yours. Are you feeling better about living in Payton?"

He gave her a cryptic look. "I would say so."

She pressed. "I mean, besides our relationship and everything, do you feel like you're part of Payton yet?"

"Definitely," he said after a moment's pause.

"See, it just took time, huh?"

"Time and a good dose of patience."

"I saw your nurse Mary the other day at the grocery store, and she said you were as busy as Doc ever was."

"Yep, in fact, Mrs. Frazer actually called me 'Doc'

the other day," Stratton laughed. "That makes two people to call me that. I took it as a good sign."

"See, it only took a while to fit in."

"It only took a little while because I met you, silly. I don't know what would have happened if you hadn't adopted me and begun introducing me to people."

"I guess it was just fate that brought me to your office that first day we met."

"Fate, a sore foot, and a string of bad luck, which seems to have ended, by the way."

She glanced at him, surprised. "I guess so. Let's see. I have a good job, a beautiful place to live, and no major injuries, just two sore hands. I'd say in general, things definitely are looking up for me."

"Almost."

She quirked her eyebrows questioningly. "What did I forget?"

"Well, there is a little matter that needs attention."

"What's that?"

Stratton leaned closer and met her gaze. "I'd say that your love life has also improved tremendously."

Joanne bit her bottom lip. "I would agree."

He stepped closer. "In fact, I'd say it's about to get better."

Her breath caught. "How so?"

Stratton shrugged, then reached into a pocket of his barn jacket and pulled out a black velvet ring box. "I wanted to get you a ring. It doesn't seem like we're officially engaged yet."

Her eyes widened. "Oh, Stratton. I don't know what to say . . . you didn't have to go out and . . ."

"Wait a minute. I want to do this right." Stratton took a deep breath and then spoke. "You see . . . ah, growing up I learned that when a guy gives a girl a ring, it means a lot."

Joanne stared at the box. She lifted a hand to take it, then lowered it as it seemed as if Stratton was content to simply hold onto it for a while. "I learned that rings mean a lot, too."

"And, uh, I always learned that when a guy proposes marriage, it means he loves the girl very much."

Joanne's eyes widened as she met his blue gaze. She swallowed. "When a girl says yes in Payton, it means she loves him a lot, too."

"Now, I don't want there to be any misunderstandings between us. Just because I asked you while I was patching up your hands didn't mean I wasn't completely serious. When I ask a girl to marry me, it's for forever."

"That's good, because when I say yes, it's for forever, too." Joanne glanced at his expression, and then at the box again. She swallowed. "Especially when there's a ring involved."

His hand closed on the box. "Now, I should probably mention, that where I come from, no one believes in long engagements. Short ones are preferred."

"Here, too," she lied, thinking of her mother in a

bridal store. "In Payton, no one likes to be engaged for more than a month."

"That's good to know," he said slowly as he leaned closer toward her, "just so there's no misunderstandings."

His lips were so close she could hardly stand it. It took all of her concentration to continue their playful banter. "I'd hate for there to ever be any misunderstandings between us."

"All right then. I guess we better start off on the right foot, then." Stratton reached for her left hand, his thumb brushing the soft skin on the back of her hand. "So, would you marry me, Joanne?"

She nodded. "Yes, Stratton, I'll marry you."

He handed her the box. She opened it. There was a single round diamond, simply set in a thick gold band. It glinted vibrantly. It was the most beautiful ring she had ever seen.

His eyes met hers. "I love you, Joanne."

"I love you, too," she breathed as he took the ring from the box and slipped it on her finger.

Stratton wrapped his arms around her and held her close. "You know, what happens now, don't you?"

Joanne nuzzled her lips to his neck and then raised to meet his eyes. "No what?"

"Haven't you heard that when you begin to wish for things you don't think you can have . . ."

"Yes?"

"You get what you wish for," he said tenderly.

She laughed. "Now, wait a minute. I thought the saying was that you were supposed to be careful for what you wished for."

Stratton's eyes crinkled as he smiled. "And?"

Joanne paused for a moment, thinking of all the changes that had taken place in the last few weeks. "I'm so glad I wasn't careful."

His eyes lit up as he caught her play on words, and then finally closed the last few inches between them with a kiss. "I am too, Joanne, I am too."